Taiwan Mandarin:
50 Patterns Not in Your Textbook

課本沒教的
台灣華語句型

50

全新修訂版

蔡佩庭 Peiting Tsai 著

推薦序 Foreword · · · · · · · · · · · · · · · · · ·

It gives me great pleasure to see the publication of this volume, a collection of 50 patterns of the so-called Taiwanese Mandarin (TwMd). Peiting, the author, was a former MA student of mine at Shida, Taipei. This volume is not a theoretical analysis of TwMd but a pedagogical complement, yes complement not supplement, to standard training and learning in L2 Chinese, if it is the wish or need of some learners to be exposed to some localized linguistic phenomena. It's intended for learners of modern Chinese at the level of A2 (EU) competence.

Taiwanese Mandarin is a creole between standard Mandarin as spoken in Taiwan and the Southern Min dialect as spoken natively by some 75% of the Taiwanese population. It is a configuration of standard Mandarin phonetics and vocabulary plus Southern Min grammar. This configuration is true of all creoles globally. Therefore, the mixture is not peculiarly Taiwanese. Similar creoles can be observed elsewhere outside of Taiwan. Like most Han dialects spoken in China and Taiwan, Southern Min does not have a written script. Thus Taiwanese Mandarin as written locally in Taiwan is entirely arbitrary and most often transient. But this does not bother anyone. Users speak it and leave it to the various media to worry about how it is represented visually.

Taiwanese Mandarin touches hearts at the local and the deepest level. If it is important for you to be in touch with the local population in Taiwan, this book is a must. Enjoy it!!

Shou-hsin Teng
Chungyuan Christian University, Taiwan
January 25, 2022

作者序 Preface

課本沒教的台灣華語句型50

　　本書打破一般中文／華語學習課本教授標準語的傳統，真實地反映了華語在台灣的口語樣貌，更貼近台灣社會語言現況，適合所有想要了解台灣社會語言現實的人，特別是有外國友人的台灣人。

　　內容把研究台灣華語的學術論文，轉化為通俗易懂的知識，並且搭配在台灣生活可能遇到的情境例句，很適合作為語言交換的話題，部分句式也指出了台灣華語與中國普通話的差異。另外，一般母語者很難解釋清楚的常用語氣詞，本書也說明了其功能與使用情境。而透過大眾傳播媒體上經常出現的流行語句式，以及種種台語和外來語詞彙，讀者也能夠更認識台灣當代社會。

　　中文、英語、西班牙語是世界上使用人口最多的前三大語言，正如英語有英式、美式、澳洲式，西班牙語有歐洲的、拉丁美洲的，中文也有中國、台灣不同的在地性差別。所有的中文學習者幾乎都會接觸到有在地特色的華語，而透過認識有在地特色的華語，可以更深入的了解該社會。台灣是個移民社會，薈萃許多美好的人事物，有豐沛的生命力，同時，台灣的華語也無可避免地受到其他語言的影響。如果你對台灣有興趣，這本書可以幫助你認識台灣華語，藉以更理解台灣文化。

　　在海外生活多年，「鄉音」永遠是最親切、溫暖、療癒的聲音，這本書匯集了一部分「鄉音」的特徵。特別感謝 Dr. Jonathan Ludwig、林君萍、莊淑芬、鄧守信教授（依姓氏筆劃排序）等人在本書撰寫期間提供諮詢和寶貴的意見，讓本書內容更為完善。謝謝林銘珊和徐家偉為錄製音檔所投入的心力。很高興在社長王愿琦、編輯鄧元婷以及瑞蘭國際團隊盡心盡力的協助之下，這本書誕生了，謹獻給喜愛台灣的你。

2022.02.14

致讀者

:: **適用對象**

　　這本書是為了已在台灣的中文學習者、有意到台灣生活、旅遊的人、台灣人的外國友人,以及想教外國友人中文的台灣人而寫。希望透過學習本書的內容能與台灣人溝通更順暢,並且更了解台灣社會。本書適合基礎級以上的中文學習者,也就是具備台灣華語文能力測驗 (TOCFL) 基礎級、中國 2021 年新版漢語水平考試 (HSK) 基礎三級、歐洲共同語文參考架構 (CEFR) A2 級、美國外語教學委員會 (ACTFL) 中級中等 (Intermediate-mid) 程度,或美國跨部門語言圓桌量表(Interagency Language Roundtable scale) 1+ 級,在學過一定數量的標準中文以後,進一步認識一些台灣的在地用法。本書可以作為自學教材,也可以作為中文課的補充材料。對於偏向訓練聽說的商務人士,也可以跟著例句音檔學習。本書也可以增加台灣以外的華語人士對台灣語言特色與時事的了解,對於機器翻譯、自然語言處理的程式設計師、外籍記者和外交工作人員,以及對外漢語教學的教育者同樣有助益。

To The Reader ·

This book is written for Mandarin Chinese learners who are already in Taiwan, those who intend to live or travel in Taiwan, foreign friends of Taiwanese, and Taiwanese who want to teach Mandarin to their foreign friends. This book will help the readers learn more about Taiwan Mandarin and Taiwan, and be able to communicate better with Taiwanese. It is good for Mandarin Chinese learners of the basic level, that is, the basic level of the Test of Chinese as Foreign Language (TOCFL) in Taiwan, Level 3 in the new version of the Chinese Proficiency Test in China (Hànyǔ Shuǐpíng Kǎoshì, HSK) 2021, A2 level in the Common European Framework of Reference for Languages (CEFR), Intermediate-mid level in the American Council on the Teaching of Foreign Languages (ACTFL) or 1+ level in Interagency Language Roundtable scale (ILR). After reaching the basic level and having acquired a certain amount of standard Mandarin, one may learn some local usages in Taiwan. In this regard, this book can be used as a self-study textbook or as a supplement to a Mandarin Chinese class. Business professionals, who prefer listening and speaking training, can learn by following the accompanying audio. This book will also help Chinese speakers outside Taiwan understand Taiwan Mandarin features and current local affairs. It is also helpful for programmers of machine translation and natural language processing, foreign journalists, diplomatic staff, and educators of Chinese as a second language.

致讀者

主要內容

　　本書以中英雙語的方式介紹五十個使用頻率高，但一般中文教科書沒有收錄的台灣在地華語口語句型。這些口語並不是學校教育規範的標準語，但卻是許多台灣人日常生活的一部分，並且隨著網路與影視作品的傳播，有的也漸漸擴散到其他的華語區。本書內容一共分為五個部分，包括台灣華語句式、語氣助詞、流行語句型、台語詞彙和外來語詞彙。收錄的內容主要是不同於中國普通話的口語用法，有些也常見於媒體書面文字。標音方面，為了學習者的方便，採用多數中文學習者比較熟悉的漢語拼音，台語詞彙也是以漢語拼音標注。例句中的詞彙，除了「第三單元：流行語句型」需要搭配時事相關的詞彙，所以可能難度較高以外，大致依據華語文能力測驗會公布的華語八千詞基礎級以下詞彙表選詞，且例句情境多樣、實際。每三或四個句型之後有一個綜合練習，讓學習者可以檢驗學習成果。

To The Reader

Using Chinese and English texts, this book introduces 50 frequently used Mandarin sentence patterns, which are not found in general Chinese textbooks but are spoken locally in Taiwan. These patterns are not authorized standard Mandarin, but they are an essential part of the daily lives of many Taiwanese. Some of them have also been gradually spreading to other Chinese-speaking areas through the Internet, movies, and television shows. The content has five parts: Taiwan Mandarin sentence patterns, modal particles, catch phrase patterns, Taiwanese morphemes, and loan morphemes. The content is about colloquial usages and differences from Chinese Mandarin. Some are also commonly found in written texts in the media. In terms of pronunciation transcription, Hanyu Pinyin is adopted for the convenience of most Mandarin Chinese learners, and Taiwanese vocabulary is also transcribed in Pinyin. As for vocabulary used in the examples, except for the more advanced sample sentences in Part III – with catch phrase patterns that need to collocate with vocabulary related to current affairs – they are generally chosen from the 8000-word list published by the TOCFL, and the example sentences are with various situations and practical. After every three or four sentence patterns, there will be a review exercise so learners can check their learning results.

致讀者 ･･･････････････････････

::

本書特色

　　許多人都知道台灣華語與中國普通話有發音、詞彙上的差異，對此學術上也有相當多的研究。但是很少有專門為華語學習者在句法上說明兩者差異的書籍，更少有介紹台灣在地口語句型的專書。台灣、中國以及海外所出版的中文教材，以及各個語言學習機構教授的都是規範的標準語，然而台灣在地的華語口語與規範的標準語卻不完全相同。在學校或語言學習機構學習過中文的外國人常常發現雖然在台灣溝通沒有障礙，但是自己所說的中文往往過於正式，表達方式與台灣人稍有距離感。希望透過本書的介紹，讓中文學習者有能力以接近台灣人的語言風格與台灣人交流，讓在地人覺得親切自然，進而讓中文學習者跟台灣人的互動交談更加順利愉快。

To The Reader

Many people know that Taiwan Mandarin and Chinese Mandarin have some differences in pronunciation and vocabulary, and there have been quite a few academic studies about them. However, differences at the syntactic level are rarely introduced to Chinese language learners, let alone making them aware of colloquial patterns in Taiwan Mandarin. Chinese textbooks published in China, Taiwan, and elsewhere, as well as Chinese offered at language-learning institutions around the world, teach official standard Mandarin, which is not exactly the same as the Mandarin spoken in Taiwan. Foreigners who have studied Mandarin in schools or at language learning institutions often find that the Mandarin they speak is too formal, and their expressions are somehow distant from Taiwanese though they usually do not have trouble communicating with locals in Taiwan. I hope this book can help Mandarin learners be able to communicate with Taiwanese in the fashion that is close to the locals so they will feel and come off as more friendly and natural, and so that interactions between foreigners and Taiwanese will be smoother and more enjoyable.

凡例 ·····························

本書所指的台灣華語是在台灣使用的華語，不限於學術界所定義「規範的台灣國語」，也包含日常使用的口語。全書以中英雙語呈現，但有鑑於語言無法完全對等，英文翻譯僅供文意參考，文句標點依中、英語各自的慣例，例句部分請不要逐字逐句比對學習。部分中文詞彙提供必要的「字面意英文」置於引號 ‘ ’ 中，中文的短語和句子的「英文語意翻譯」則是置於括弧（ ） 中，以利學習。書中採用漢語拼音標注台灣在地口語發音，與辭典的字詞標音未必完全相同。內容包含以下的結構：

:: **情境例句／原文例句**

情境例句是用對話的方式呈現句型，模擬真實使用情況。「第三單元：流行語句型」則是收錄該流行語句型中，最先開始廣泛使用的原始句子。

:: **句型／結構說明**

句型／結構說明是將同類的句子或詞彙拆解開來分析，而得到其組成的關鍵成份。實際使用的時候可以加上

Introduction ·······························

Taiwan Mandarin in this book refers to the Mandarin spoken in Taiwan. It is not limited to the standard Mandarin used in Taiwan as defined by academic circle, and it includes the spoken Mandarin used in daily life. The content of this book is presented in both Chinese and English. However, because the languages are not completely equivalent, the English translation is for textual reference only. The punctuation in sentences is in accordance with the conventions of Chinese and English respectively. Please do not study the example sentences word by word between the two languages. To help learning, some Chinese words are given literal English translations in quotation marks ' ', and the translation of phrases and sentences are set in parentheses ( ). In this book, Hanyu Pinyin is adopted to indicate how the words are pronounced colloquially in Taiwan. They are not necessarily identical as shown in the dictionary. The content contains the following structure:

:: **Contextual Example / Original Example**

Contextual sentences are examples of sentence patterns presented in dialogue form to simulate authentic usage. In Part III, Catch Phrase Patterns, examples show the texts where the pattern originated.

:: **Sentence Pattern / Structure**

The description of a sentence pattern or a compound structure comes from analyzing sentences or words in the same

凡例 ....

副詞、時間詞等等。句型公式細節請詳見第 17 頁說明。詞類的縮略語請詳見第 18 頁的縮語表。

:: 用法

解釋使用該句型的情況和意義，以及其他應該注意的事項。

:: 例句

本書提供的例句有單句也有對話，包含邀請、道歉、打招呼、告別、感謝等等社交情境。單句是完整的句子，對話的例句，如同真實語境，如果對話雙方都知道談話當中所指是什麼，是經常省略的，多數是主語或者賓語。例如：我要趕快 [把你說的] 寫起來，要不然會忘記。此外，例句內容能成為與母語者談論的話題，藉以促進中高級程度的學習者練習成段表達。

Introduction

patterns. It is then composed of the key elements. In actual use, it can add adverbs, time words, etc. The details of pattern formulae are shown on page 17. For abbreviations of parts of speech, please refer to the abbreviation table on page 18.

:: Usage

This section explains the applicable situation and meaning in which to use the sentence pattern, as well as the matters that should be given attention.

:: Example

The examples provided in this book include single sentences and dialogues. The scenarios consider all kinds of social situations, such as invitation, apology, greeting, farewell, appreciation, etc. If the example is a single sentence, it is a complete sentence. If the example is a dialogue, it is just like authentic content, that is to say, if both parties in the dialogue know what they are talking about in the conversation, the referred nouns are often omitted, most likely subject or object. For example: Wǒ yào gǎnkuài [bǎ nǐ shuō de] xiě qǐlái, yàobùrán huì wàngjì. (I want to write [what you said] as soon as possible, or I will forget it.) The content of the examples can also be topics for discussion with native speakers to give intermediate and advanced learners practice expressions in paragraphs.

凡例 ∙∙

∷ **原來如此／你知道嗎**

補充句型相關的語文知識或者是文化短文，也可以作為中高級程度的閱讀材料。

∷ **出處**

在第三單元中，介紹流行語的起源、背景，並提供兩個重點詞彙，幫助中高級程度學習者增加詞彙。

∷ **練習**

每三或四個句型之後安排一個綜合練習，解答列在附錄。每個練習的最後提供一個沒有標準答案的「挑戰你自己」的小單元，學習者可以向母語者詢問自己的回答是否恰當。

∷ **音檔**

書中的所有例句（包含情境例句）與練習皆有音檔，以幫助學習者漢字識讀、發音以及流利度。在開始使用本書之前，別忘了先找到書封上的 QR Code，拿出手機掃描，就能立即下載書中所有音檔（請自行使用智慧型手機，下載喜歡的 QR Code 掃描器，更能有效偵測書中 QR Code。）

Introduction ·

:: No wonder / Do you know

This section includes supplementary language knowledge or cultural notes related to the sentence pattern. It can also be used as intermediate and advanced reading material.

:: Sourse

This section introduces the origin and background of catch phrases in Part III. Two key lexical items are provided to help intermediate and advanced learners expand their vocabulary.

:: Exercise

After every three or four sentence patterns, there is an exercise. The answer keys are provided in the appendix. At the end of each exercise is a section with open-ended questions called "Challenge yourself," where learners are encouraged to speak with native speakers to check if their answers are appropriate.

:: Audios

Every example (including the contextual examples) and every exercise in this book has an audio recording. This is to help learners' reading, pronunciation, and speaking flow. Please use a smartphone to scan the QR Code on the book cover to download the complete audios.

句型結構說明 Symbols · · · · · · · · · · · · · · ·

（　　）表示可以出現在句型中，也可以省略。
The word in ( ) may or may not be present in a sentence pattern.

以此句型為例：

Sub +（沒）有 + 要／想 + VP

／表示可以使用前者或後者的字。
／ indicates that the element can be either the former or the latter word.

※ 請注意：句型結構描述如果包含特定的標點符號，表示是固定的用法。如果沒有包含特定的標點符號，表示是開放的用法，有多種可能，句子可以是問句、陳述句等等。中 表示普通話的用法。台 表示台灣華語的用法。

※ Note: If the sentence structure description contains a specific punctuation mark, it indicates a fixed expression. If it does not include a specific punctuation mark, it means that it has an open expression. There are many possibilities. The sentence can be a question, a statement, etc. 中 indicates an expression in Pǔtōnghuà; 台 indicates an expression in Táiwān Huáyǔ.

縮語表 Abbreviation of Terms

Abbr	Full	中文	Example
N	Noun	名詞	魚、名字、辦公室、晚飯、生日、昨天
V	Verb (all kinds)	動詞	睡、騎、開、覺得、高興、想
V_{act}	Action Verb	動作動詞	坐、跑、站、告訴、看、踢、說
V_{st}	Stative Verb	狀態動詞	聰明、漂亮、喜歡、知道、高、大
S	Sentence	句子	我昨天看了兩本書。
			媽媽包的餃子好吃嗎？
			請坐下。
Sub	Subject	主語	媽媽今天包餃子。
			我昨天看了兩本書。
Obj	Object	賓語	媽媽包餃子。
			我看了兩本書。
VP	Verb Phrase	動詞短語	包餃子
			看了兩本書
NP	Noun Phrase	名詞短語	很好吃的餃子
			很有趣的書

※ 請注意：「漂亮、高、大」等對譯成英文是形容詞，但是為了避免「* 她是漂亮。」這種錯誤的句子，這裡不歸類為形容詞，而是狀態動詞。

※Note: "piàoliàng (beautiful), gāo (tall), dà (big)" are not categorized as adjectives as they are in English in order to avoid such incorrect sentences like "*tā shì piàoliàng. (She is beautiful.)" Instead, they are classified as stative verbs.

目次
Table of Contents

第一單元：台灣華語句式
Part I: Taiwan Mandarin Sentence Patterns

第二單元：語氣助詞
Part II: Modal Particles

目次
Table of Contents

第三單元：流行語句型
Part III: Catch Phrase Patterns

第四單元：台語詞彙
Part IV: Taiwanese Morphemes

目次
Table of Contents

如何掃描 QR Code 下載音檔

1. 以手機內建的相機或是掃描 QR Code 的 App 掃描封面的 QR Code。
2. 點選「雲端硬碟」的連結之後，進入音檔清單畫面，接著點選畫面右上角的「三個點」。
3. 點選「新增至「已加星號」專區」一欄，星星即會變成黃色或黑色，代表加入成功。
4. 開啟電腦，打開您的「雲端硬碟」網頁，點選左側欄位的「已加星號」。
5. 選擇該音檔資料夾，點滑鼠右鍵，選擇「下載」，即可將音檔存入電腦。

How to scan QR Code to download audio files

1. Scan the QR Code on the cover by using the camera or any scanning App on your smartphone.
2. After opening your Cloud Drive, you will see the list of audios files. Click the three dots on the upper right corner.
3. Click Add to Starred, the stars will turn yellow or black.
4. Turn on your computer, open your Cloud Drive, and then click Starred on the left pane.
5. Right click on the audio folder, and then click download.

台灣華語句式

　　華語、國語、漢語、普通話、中國話、中文指的是同一種語言，都是英文的 Mandarin Chinese，只是在不同地方、對不同人使用不同名詞，詞彙、語法、發音在不同地方也有些差異。對非華人來說這個語言是華語、中國話、中文。在台灣因為這個語言是國家的官方語言，因此把它叫做「國語」，直到 2019 年通過國家語言發展法，國語才不再限於華語。而中國是多民族國家，其中「漢族」是人口最多的，所以把漢族人說的語言叫做「漢語」，但是嚴格來說廣東話、閩南話、上海話等漢語方言也都是漢語。中國用這個以北京話為基礎的漢語作為跨民族、跨方言區的溝通語言，所以把它叫做「普通話」。本書把在台灣使用的叫做「台灣華語」來相對於在中國所稱的「普通話」。這裡所列的台灣華語句式是受到台語影響而不同於普通話的十個常見句式。

Taiwan Mandarin Sentence Patterns

Huáyǔ, Guóyǔ, Hànyǔ, Pǔtōnghuà, Zhōngguóhuà, and Zhōngwén all refer to the same language, Mandarin Chinese. The term may vary depending on the target audience. There are also some differences in vocabulary, grammar, and pronunciation among places where it is spoken. To people of non-Chinese ethnicity, this language is called "Huáyǔ (the language of ethnic Chinese)", "Zhōngguóhuà (Chinese spoken language)", or "Zhōngwén (Chinese written language)." In Taiwan, this language is called "Guóyǔ (national language)" because it was the official language of the nation until the Development of National Language Act was passed in 2019: national languages are no longer limited to Mandarin. In China, where the Han people are the most populous among all the ethnic groups, it is called "Hànyǔ (Han language)" because it is the language spoken by the Han people. Strictly speaking, however, Cantonese, Southern Min / Hokkien, Shanghainese, and other dialects are "Hànyǔ" as well. "Pǔtōnghuà (common language)" is based on the Beijing dialect and is used to communicate across ethnic and dialect boundaries in China. In this book, the Mandarin used in Taiwan is called "Táiwān Huáyǔ" as opposed to "Pǔtōnghuà" used in China hereafter. Here are ten common Taiwan Mandarin sentence patterns that are affected by the language Taiwanese and are different from Pǔtōnghuà.

:: **情境例句 Contextual Example** 🎧 MP3-001

A：你來台灣三個月了，有喝過台灣啤酒嗎？

A：You have been in Taiwan for three months. Have you tried Taiwan Beer?

B：有啊，我到台灣的第一個星期六就喝了兩瓶。

B：Yes, I have. I drank two bottles on my first Saturday in Taiwan.

:: **句型 Sentence Pattern**

1｜Sub ＋（沒）有＋ VP
2｜Sub ＋（沒）有＋要／想＋ VP
3｜Sub ＋（沒）有＋在＋ VP
4｜Sub ＋ 有沒有＋ VP ？

普通話句型 Compare with Pǔtōnghuà

Sub ＋ VP ＋了 　　　Sub ＋ V ＋過＋ Obj

問句 Sub ＋ VP ＋了＋沒有？ Sub ＋ V ＋過＋ Obj+ 沒有？

中 你看見我的手機了沒有？ 我喝過台灣啤酒。
台 你有沒有看到我的手機？ 我有喝過台灣啤酒。
Have you seen my phone? I've had Taiwanese beer.

:: **用法 Usage**

　　這個句型用在口語，要表達的是：1）表示動作完成；2）表示事件的常態，如果表達的是個人常態性的行為，所指的就是一個人的習慣；3）在搭配「想」、「要」、「想要」或狀態動詞時，表示某個存在的事實。

　　For colloquial expressions, this pattern conveys 1) a completed action; 2) a habitual

課本沒教的台灣華語句型50

event – if the event is about an individual's behavior, it refers to a habit. 3) an existing fact when the pattern collocates with xiǎng 'to think', yào 'to want', xiǎngyào 'would like to', or a stative verb.

:: **例句 Example**

🎧 MP3-002

1 ｜ 完成	**1 ｜ completed action**
1.1｜ 我有買到去台東的火車票，你呢？	1.1｜ I got the train ticket to Taitung. How about you?
1.2｜ 他出國以後，都沒有寫信給我，是把我忘了吧？	1.2｜ He never wrote me a letter after he went abroad. Did he forget me?
1.3｜ 你去了那麼久，有沒有借到課本啊？	1.3｜ You've been gone for so long. Did you get the textbook?
2 ｜ 事件的常態	**2 ｜ habitual event**
2.1｜ 我爸爸年輕的時候有抽煙。	2.1｜ My dad smoked when he was young.
2.2｜ 我先生以前有喝酒，因為身體不好，現在不喝了。	2.2｜ My husband used to drink. Because of poor health, he does not drink now.
2.3｜ 這家店沒有賣咖啡，只有賣茶。	2.3｜ This shop doesn't sell coffee but tea.
2.4｜ 雖然工作很忙，但是我還有在學英文。	2.4｜ Although my job is busy, I still keep learning English.
3 ｜ 存在的事實	**3 ｜ existing fact**
3.1｜ 我兒子有想要開公司，所以畢業以後一直沒去找工作。	3.1｜ My son wants to start a company, so he has never looked for a job after graduation.
3.2｜ 你有那麼累嗎？不能換了衣服再睡覺嗎？	3.2｜ Are you really that tired? Can't you go to bed after changing clothes?
3.3｜ 我覺得今天沒有很冷。	3.3｜ For me, it's not very cold today.

3.4 | 禮拜天我有要去機場接爺爺，你有沒有要去？

3.4 | I am going to the airport to pick up Grandpa. Do you want to go?

！原來如此 No Wonder

　　大航海時代，荷屬東印度公司航行到台灣經商，並且建立政權（1624-1662年），也招募漢人協同開發，當時台灣已有少數漢人移民和原住民族居住。1662-1683 年，大批漢人移民隨著鄭成功到台灣來避難開墾。這批漢人大多來自中國福建南部，後來也有少部分來自廣東的移民。來自福建的說閩南話，來自廣東的說客家話。 1895 年甲午戰爭清朝戰敗，把台灣割讓給日本之後，台灣開始了五十年的日治時期直到 1945 年二次世界大戰結束，於是日語逐漸成了台灣通行的語言，閩南語也因此增加了許多日語詞彙，加上之前少部分的原住民語、荷語詞彙而形成今日的台語。

　　中華民國政府從 1913 年起，就努力在中國推行以北京話為基礎的「國語運動」，但是當時台灣是仍是日本的領土，台灣的「國語教育」是學習日語。第二次世界大戰結束以後，中國繼續內戰，後來國民黨敗給共產黨，1949 年國民黨政府遷到台灣，積極推廣中文的「國語運動」，甚至一度在學校禁說方言、限制方言節目在電視播出的時數來推廣「國語」。不過，語言是活的，就像人會受到環境或是朋友的影響一樣，台灣人說的國語在長時間接觸台語的情況下，漸漸發展出和中國普通話有些差別的台灣華語。然而隨著兩岸交流頻繁以及影視作品的流通，台灣華語在中國也偶爾聽得到，甚至擴散傳播到其他的華語圈，像是新加坡、馬來西亞、香港和澳門等地。

　　In the Age of Discovery, the Dutch East India Company came to Formosa, a.k.a. Taiwan, and established its rule for trading (1624-1662). During this period, Han Chinese were recruited to develop the island. Before that time, aboriginals and a small number of Han already lived on the island. From 1662 to 1683, many more Han arrived as refugees or immigrated to Taiwan with Koxinga. Most of them were from southern Fujian province and spoke Southern Hokkien. More from Guangdong province arrived later; they spoke Hakka. After the Sino-Japanese War ended in 1895, Taiwan was ceded to Japan, which colonized it over the next 50 years until the end of World War II (WWII) in 1945. Japanese gradually became the common language in Taiwan during this time. Therefore, Southern Hokkien was enriched with words from Japanese, as well as Aboriginal languages and Dutch to make contemporary Taiwanese.

　　Since 1913, the government of the Republic of China had been trying to promote the "National Language Movement" in China. The "national language" was Mandarin, based on the Beijing dialect, but Taiwan was still a Japanese territory and "National Language Education" in Taiwan required learning Japanese at that time. After WWII, the civil war in China resumed, and the Kuomintang (KMT) was later defeated by the Communists. In 1949, the KMT government self-exiled to Taiwan and then aggressively promoted Mandarin as the "national language" in Taiwan. The government prohibited dialects from being spoken at school and limited broadcasting of dialects on TV for decades. However, just as a person will be changed by friends or surroundings, Mandarin in Taiwan has been changed by Taiwanese speakers over the years. Taiwan Mandarin is not exactly the same as Mandarin in China today, but it can still be occasionally heard in China because of pop culture and people traveling frequently across the Taiwan Strait. It has even spread to other Chinese speaking communities, including Singapore, Malaysia, Hong Kong, and Macao.

:: **情境例句 Contextual Example**　　　🎧 MP3-003

A：爸爸去台中工作只有一個星
　　期，怎麼帶這麼多衣服？

B：他擔心說到了那邊不能洗衣
　　服。

A：Dad works in Taichung just for one
　　week. Why does he bring so many
　　clothes?

B：He is worried that he won't be able
　　to do his laundry after he gets there.

:: **句型 Sentence Pattern**

1 | Sub ＋ V$_{act}$ ＋說＋ S
2 | Topic ＋不會／沒有／哪有＋說＋ V$_{st}$

:: **用法 Usage**

　　句型 1 的「說」做為補語標誌，類似英文子句前的「that」，後面接一個子
句。句型 2 的主題一般是名詞短語，「說」標誌主題的狀態。

　　In Pattern 1, "shuō" is used as a complementary marker, similar to "that" before a
clause in English, and then is followed by a clause. The topic in Pattern 2 is usually a
noun phrase, and "shuō" indicates the state of the topic.

:: **例句 Example**　　　🎧 MP3-004

1 | 句型 1

1.1 | 我想說你今天不來了，所以才
　　　沒準備你的麵包跟飲料。

1.2 | 要是你們七月來台灣，就可以
　　　知道說台灣的夏天有多熱。

1 | Pattern 1

1.1 | I thought that you were not coming
　　　today. That's why I didn't prepare
　　　your bread and drink.

1.2 | If you come to Taiwan in July, you
　　　will know how hot it is in Taiwan in
　　　summer.

2 ｜ 句型 2

2.1 ｜ 這種水果不會說很酸，你可以試試看。

2.2 ｜ 上次我們住的旅館沒有說很差，你有興趣的話，我可以給你他們的電話。

2.3 ｜ 一支手錶兩萬塊錢哪有說很便宜？

2 ｜ Pattern 2

2.1 ｜ This kind of fruit is not sour. You can try it.

2.2 ｜ The hotel we stayed at last time was not all bad. I can give you their phone number if you're interested.

2.3 ｜ NT$20,000 for a watch?! That's not cheap!

！你知道嗎 Do you know

「說」做為補語標誌的用法，在普通話中也有，例如：「現在很多人不想結婚，是因為覺得說一個人也很好。」「我覺得說……」在口語中也很常見。但是這種用法的「說」搭配的動詞只限於「覺得、認為、以為、想」等表達意見類的，「說」在這裡帶有動詞性「報導」的意思。另外，普通話和台灣華語也都會在「如果、或是、比方、雖然、所以、但是、也就是、像、無論、不管」等連接詞後加上「說」，例如：「不管說我前一天晚上幾點睡，第二天一定八點以前就起來。」

The use of "shuō" as a complementary marker is also found in Pǔtōnghuà. For example, "Xiànzài hěn duō rén bù xiǎng jiéhūn, shì yīnwèi juéde shuō yí ge rén yě hěn hǎo. (Nowadays, many people don't want to get married because they think it's nice to be single.)" "wǒ juéde shuō…. 'I think that…'" is also very common in colloquial expressions. However, the verbs used in this way are limited to those for expressing opinions such as juéde, rènwéi, yǐwéi, xiǎng (all meaning 'think') where "shuō" has the verbal meaning of "report." In addition, both Pǔtōnghuà and Táiwān Huáyǔ also add "shuō" after the conjunction "ruóguǒ 'if', huòshì 'or', bǐfāng 'for example', suīrán 'though', suǒyǐ 'therefore', dànshì 'but', yě jiùshì 'that is to say', xiàng 'like', wúlùn 'whether', bùguǎn 'despite'." For example, "Bùguǎn shuō wǒ qián yì tiān wǎnshàng jǐ diǎn shuì, dì èr tiān yídìng bā diǎn yǐqián jiù qǐlái. (No matter what time I go to bed the night before, I will be up by 8:00 the next day.)"

03 給 + N + V gěi sentence

:: **情境例句 Contextual Example** 🎧 MP3-005

A：站著等很久了吧？這裡給你坐。

B：謝謝你，我不累，站著就好。

A：You have been standing for a long time, right? Take this seat.

B：Thank you, I'm not tired, I'm fine standing.

:: **句型 Sentence Pattern**

1 | 給 + N + V_{act}
2 | 給 + N + V_{st}
3 | 給 + N + V_{act}
4 | Sub + 給 + Obj + V_{act}
5 | Obj……+ 給他 + VP
6 | 給他／它 + VP

:: **用法 Usage**

　句型 1 和句型 2 的「給」是讓、使的意思，「給」後面接的名詞是人或動物。

　句型 3 的「給」是跟、向的意思，「給」後面接的名詞是動作的來源。

　句型 4 的動詞只能是動作動詞，而動詞對象的賓語接在「給」的後面。

　句型 5 動作對象的賓語在「給」的前面，用代名詞「他」來代表前面的賓語，然後接動詞短語。

　句型 6 的「給他／它」沒有特別的意義，一般是年輕人與親近的朋友聊天、開玩笑、發表意見的時候故意說出來的。如果不說「給他／它」完全不影響句子的意思，說出來增加了親切、鄉土的語氣。「給他／它」後面接的動詞短語，可以是一個狀態動詞，也可以是動作動詞加補語。

　In Pattern 1 and Pattern 2, "gěi" means to "let" or "make," and nouns following "gěi" are people or animals.

　In Pattern 3, "gěi" means "from" or "toward." The noun following "gěi" is the source of the action.

In Pattern 4, the only verb allowed is an action verb, and the object of the verb is followed by "gěi."

In Pattern 5, the object of the action verb is in front of "gěi." The pronoun "tā" is used to represent the object, and then the verb phrase is followed.

In Pattern 6, "gěitā" has no specific meaning. It is usually deliberately spoken by young people when chatting, joking, or expressing opinions with close friends. If you do not say "gěitā", it will not affect the meaning of the sentence at all. If you say it, it will give a cordial and rural tone. The verb phrase following "gěitā" can be a stative verb or an action verb with a complement.

:: **例句 Example**

🎧 MP3-006

1 | 句型 1

1.1 | 中午吃什麼給你決定。

1.2 | 你已經玩球玩了兩個鐘頭了，
現在給弟弟玩吧。

1 | Pattern 1

1.1 | You decide what we eat for lunch.

1.2 | You've been playing with the ball for two hours. Now give it to your younger brother.

2 | 句型 2

2.1 | 我說個笑話給大家開心一下。

2.2 | 這件衣服打八五折賣你，給你
便宜一點。

2 | Pattern 2

2.1 | Let me tell a joke to make everyone happy.

2.2 | This dress will be sold to you at a 15% discount. It's cheaper for you.

3 | 句型 3

3.1 | 阿樂給公司借了很多錢，但是
都沒還。

3.2 | 吃多少拿多少，不要給人家拿
那麼多菜，吃不完就浪費了。

3 | Pattern 3

3.1 | A Le borrowed a lot of money from the company, but didn't pay back at all.

3.2 | Take as much as you can eat. Don't take too much. It will be wasted if you can't finish it.

4 | 句型 4

4.1 | 你的朋友不會中文，去台灣以前你要給他上課。

4.2 | 問我這麼難的事，你是在給我考試嗎？

5 | 句型 5

5.1 | 如果你不喜歡白色的牆，那就給他換成別的顏色嘛。

5.2 | 送你的生日禮物趕快給他打開啊。

6 | 句型 6

6.1 | 走！我們去慶祝你找到工作，去好好給他喝兩杯。

6.2 | 太久沒見到你，給他忘了你的生日了。

4 | Pattern 4

4.1 | Your friend doesn't know how to speak Chinese. Before he goes to Taiwan, you need to teach him.

4.2 | You ask me such a difficult question. Are you giving me a test?

5 | Pattern 5

5.1 | If you don't like the white wall, just change it to another color.

5.2 | Hurry up and open the birthday present that I am giving you.

6 | Pattern 6

6.1 | Let's go celebrate you getting a job and have a good drink.

6.2 | It's been too long since I saw you. I have forgotten your birthday.

❗ 你知道嗎 Do you know

　　上面列的六種「給」的句型大多是受到台語影響演變出來的用法，但是句型 1 中「給」相當於「使／讓」的用法普通話也有，不過只能搭配「看、聽、用、吃」等之類的動作動詞，不能搭配「方便、高興、快、慢」等之類的狀態動詞。另外，普通話和台灣華語都有「Sub ＋給我＋ VP」這樣的句型，例如：「房間裡面有人在睡覺，你們幾個孩子給我安靜一點。」一般是在說話人生氣或命令別人時候說的句子。

The six patterns listed here mostly evolved from Taiwanese language influence. However, the usage of "gěi" in Pattern 1 also exists in Pǔtōnghuà, but it can only be collocated with action verbs such as kàn 'see', tīng 'listen', yòng 'use', chī 'eat' and cannot be collocated with stative verbs, such as fāngbiàn 'convenient', gāoxìng 'happy', kuài 'fast', and màn 'slow'. In addition, the pattern "Sub+gěi wǒ+VP" exists both in Pǔtōnghuà and Táiwān Huáyǔ. For example, "Fángjiān lǐmiàn yǒu rén zài shuìjiào, nǐmen jǐ ge háizi gěi wǒ ānjìng yì diǎn. (Someone is sleeping in the room. You kids, be quiet.)" It is usually said when the speaker is angry or giving a command.

I. 用（）裡的詞把句子變換成台灣華語的表達方式：

Use the words in ( ) to transform the sentences into expressions of Táiwān Huáyǔ:

例 你認識會說日語的人嗎？（有） → 你有認識會說日語的人嗎？

1｜他那麼想去，就帶他去吧。（給）

2｜我今天才發現大房子打掃起來又累又花時間。（說）

3｜她非常喜歡吃水果，不管吃得多飽，什麼水果都還能吃下去。(給他)

4｜台北的交通哪有很不方便？（說）

5｜阿新小學的時候打籃球，所以現在特別高。（有）

6｜每天洗完臉以後，用這一瓶，三個月以後就能使你年輕五歲。（給）

7｜我們公司要不要參加這個計畫，你星期四要跟老闆報告。（給）

8｜公園離這裡沒有很遠，走路就能到了。（說）

9｜我參觀過你們學校了，我就在學校的書店等你吧。（有）

10｜那個座位是讓老人或者不方便的人坐的。（給）

II. 填空
Fill in the blank:

a 有 | b 沒有 | c 說 | d 給 | e 給他

1 | A：上次你請我吃飯，今天 ＿＿＿＿ 我請。

    B：那我就不客氣了。

2 | A：時間 ＿＿＿＿ 過得好快，暑假明天就要結束了。唉～

    B：是啊，我還沒玩夠呢。

3 | A：這件褲子你 ＿＿＿＿ 喜歡嗎？

    B：還不錯，就是有點貴。

4 | A：你去看的那個房子怎麼樣？要租嗎？

    B：房子還算新，附近也 ＿＿＿＿ 很吵，而且房租不會 ＿＿＿＿ 很貴。
    我決定租了。

▶ 挑戰你自己：用「有／給／說」的句型繼續上面任何一個對話。
Challenge yourself: Continue any of the above conversations with the sentence pattern of yǒu / gěi / shuō.

04 在 + V zài sentence

:: **情境例句 Contextual Example** 🎧 MP3-008

A：請問這附近哪裡有在賣花？

B：前面路口右轉就有一家花店。

A：May I ask where I can buy flowers around here?

B：Turn right at the intersection ahead and a flower shop is just right there.

:: **句型 Sentence Pattern**

1｜Sub ＋（平常／每天／時間）＋沒有／有＋在＋ V
2｜Sub ＋在＋ V$_{st}$
3｜NP ＋是＋……的時候＋在＋ V$_{act}$ ＋的
4｜在＋ VP

:: **用法 Usage**

「在＋V」表示某種活動或者狀態的持續。句型 1 與「有」字句相同，表示事實或是習慣、態度的存在。句型 2 表示某種狀態的持續。句型 3 表示某種東西的用途。句型 4 表示職業。

"zài + V" indicates that a certain action is in progress or that a certain state is ongoing. Pattern 1 is the same as the "yǒu sentence" pattern. It expresses the continuation of an activity or state, in other words, the existence of a fact, habit or attitude. Pattern 2 expresses the continuation of a state. Pattern 3 explains the use of something. Pattern 4 describes an occupation.

:: **例句 Example** 🎧 MP3-009

1｜句型 1

1.1｜我平常都沒有在看電視新聞。

1.2｜為了參加鋼琴比賽，他每天都有在練習。

1｜Pattern 1

1.1｜I usually don't watch TV news.

1.2｜In order to enter a piano contest, he practices every day.

1.3 | 雖然 Covid-19 大流行，還是有很多人沒在怕，出門也不戴口罩。

1.3 | Despite the Covid-19 pandemic, many people are not afraid and do not wear masks when they go out.

2 | 句型 2

2.1 | 他旅行回來以後，就一直在生病，已經兩個星期了，還沒有好。

2.2 | 十一月了，南部還在熱嗎？

2 | Pattern 2

1.1 | He has been ill since he came back from the trip. It has been two weeks, and he hasn't recovered.

1.2 | It's November. Is it still hot in the south?

3 | 句型 3

3.1 | 這個藥是發燒的時候在吃的，不是肚子痛的時候在吃的。

3.2 | 這種書是我無聊的時候在看的。

3 | Pattern 3

3.1 | This medicine is for a fever, not for a stomach ache.

3.2 | This kind of book is what I read when I'm bored.

4 | 句型 4

4.1 | 他高中畢業以後就在開計程車。

4.2 | 你爸爸在教書喔？

4 | Pattern 4

4.1 | He has been driving a taxi ever since graduating high school.

4.2 | Is your father a teacher?

！你知道嗎 Do you know

　　「在」在中文教科書裡的語法說明裡有一個主要的功能，就是搭配動作動詞，表示某一個動作在進行中，或是某一個狀態在持續，也可用「正」或「正在」，例如「孩子（正）在睡覺，你小聲一點。」但要注意的是，「在」用於描述「可以反覆進行或者持續一段比較長時間的活動」，而「正在」卻不能這樣使用。所以不能說「＊一直正在注意」，但是可以說「一直在注意」。

　　In Mandarin language textbooks, the major function of "zài" is to collocate with action verbs to indicate that a certain action is in progress or that a certain state is ongoing. "zhèng" or "zhèngzài" also play the same function, e.g., "Háizi (zhèng) zài shuìjiào, nǐ xiǎo shēng yì diǎn. (The child is sleeping, please keep your voice down.)"

However, "zài" is used for repeatable activities or activities lasting for a longer period of time, but "zhèngzài" is not. You cannot say, "*yìzhí zhèngzài zhùyì", but you can say "yìzhí zài zhùyì (always pay attention)."

NOTE

第一單元：台灣華語句式
PART I: Taiwan Mandarin Sentence Patterns

:: **情境例句 Contextual Example**　　🎧 MP3-010

A：十二點半了，一起來去吃飯囉。

B：你們先去吧。我把這些做完再去吃。

A：It's 12:30. Let's go for lunch together.

B：You go ahead. I'll go eat after getting these done.

:: **句型 Sentence Pattern**

1｜來去＋ VP
2｜來去＋ N ＋（VP）

:: **用法 Usage**

　　「來去」只有「去」的意思，表示行動的意向，主語經常是我或者我們，但不出現主語時，有說話人邀約聽話人的用意。句型 2「來去」後面的名詞是目的地，後面可以接活動動詞短語，來描述在目的地要進行的活動，也可以沒有。

　　"láiqù 'come-go'" only means "qù", indicating the intention to act. The subject is often "I" or "we." When the sentence has no subject, it means that the speaker intends to invite the listener to do something. In Pattern 2, the noun following "láiqù" is a destination place. An activity phrase can follow the place noun to denote the activity at the destination, but it is optional.

:: **例句 Example**　　🎧 MP3-011

1｜**句型 1**

1.1｜報告做完了，我要來去運動一下。

1.2｜今天星期五，下班以後來去跳舞吧。

1｜**Pattern 1**

1.1｜The report is done. I'm going to exercise.

1.2｜Today is Friday. Let's go dancing after work.

2 ｜ 句型 2

2.1 ｜ 下個週末來去鄉下住一晚怎麼樣？

2.2 ｜ 暑假我要來去美國，你呢？

2.3 ｜ 週末要是天氣好的話，我們就來去海邊玩吧。

2 ｜ Pattern 2

2.1 ｜ How about going to the countryside for one night next weekend?

2.2 ｜ I'm going to America for summer vacation. How about you?

2.3 ｜ If the weather is good on the weekend, let's go to the beach.

❗ 你知道嗎 Do you know

　　「來去 XX」經常成為推銷某個地方的觀光標語，例如「來去遊府城」、「來去夏威夷」。像「來去」這樣，相反的兩個詞組合在一起，但意思只有其中的一個詞，是一種在中文裡常見的複合詞，例如「忘記、國家、得失、死活」，分別只有「忘、國、失、死」的意思。

　　"láiqù XX" often becomes a tourism slogan to promote a place, such as "láiqù yóu Fǔchéng (Tainan tourism campaign)", "láiqù Xiàwēiyí (Hawaii tourism campaign)." Like láiqù, two opposite words combine together, but only one holds the meaning. This is a common way to make a compound in Mandarin, such as wàngjì 'forget-remember', guójiā 'country-home', déshī 'gain-loss' and sǐhuó 'death-life'. They only mean wàng, guó, shī, sǐ respectively.

06 用 + V~act~ + 的 yòng sentence

:: **情境例句 Contextual Example** MP3-012

A：要是我去國外講英文，別人聽
　　不懂怎麼辦？

B：你可以用寫的啊。

A：What if I go abroad and others don't
　　understand my English?

B：You can write what you want to say.

:: **句型 Sentence Pattern**

1 ｜ 用＋ V~act~ ＋的
2 ｜ 用＋ V~act~ ＋的＋ VP
　　　用＋ V~act~ ＋的＋ N

:: **用法 Usage**

　　「用」後面接的動詞表示動作是「用什麼方式」進行。「用 V 的」可以像
句型 1 做為句子的主要謂語，也可以像句型 2 修飾動詞和句型 3 修飾名詞。

　　The verb following "yòng" indicates the way of acting. "yòng V de" can be used as
the main predicate in a sentence like Pattern 1. It can also modify the following verb
phrase or noun as in Pattern 2 and Pattern 3 respectively.

:: **例句 Example** MP3-013

1 ｜ 句型 1

1.1 ｜ 快遲到了，用跑的啦！

1.2 ｜ 雖然我聽不懂他說什麼，但是
　　　我可以用感覺的。我想他應該
　　　是餓了。

1 ｜ Pattern 1

1.1 ｜ We're almost late. Run!

1.2 ｜ Although I don't understand what he
　　　says, I can feel it. I think he should
　　　be hungry.

2 ｜ 句型 2

2.1 ｜ 手機現在也可以用說的打字
　　　了。

2 ｜ Pattern 2

2.1 ｜ Nowadays you can type on your
　　　mobile by speaking.

2.2	如果你怕忘了他家怎麼走，可以用畫的記下來。	2.2	If you are afraid of forgetting how to get to his house, you can take it down by drawing a map.

3 | 句型 3

3 | Pattern 3

3.1	我比較喜歡吃用烤的魚，你呢？	3.1	I prefer grilled fish. How about you?
3.2	她現在開用租的車，三年以後還可以換新的車呢。	3.2	She currently drives a leased car. After three years, she can replace it with a new car.

！你知道嗎 Do you know

　　「用 V 的」這個句型在普通話裡並沒有相對應的固定結構。「用」在普通話和台灣華語中都有動詞的用法，是「使用」的意思，後面接名詞，表示使用某種工具，例如「我用電腦學習。」「用＋來」後面可以接表示目的的動詞詞組，例如「杯子可以用來玩遊戲。」前面的名詞是後面動作的工具或手段。

The pattern "yòng V de" does not have an equivalent structure in Pǔtōnghuà. "yòng" is used as a verb in both Pǔtōnghuà and Táiwān Huáyǔ. It means "to use." It is followed by a noun to indicate a certain tool being used, e.g., "Wǒ yòng diànnǎo xuéxí. (I use a computer to learn.)" "yòng + lái" can be followed by a verb phrase indicating a purpose, e.g., "Bēizi kěyǐ yòng lái wán yóuxì. (Cups can be used to play games.)" The noun in the front is the instrument or means by which the action takes place.

I. 選出台灣華語的表達方式：
Choose the expression of Táiwān Huáyǔ:

(   ) 1 ｜ a 如果你的行李太重了，就一部分東西用寄的吧。

         b 如果你的行李過重了，就把一部分東西寄回去吧。

(   ) 2 ｜ a 這款裙子還很流行嗎？我媽年輕的時候穿過這種裙子呢。

         b 這種裙子還在流行嗎？這不是我媽年輕的時候在穿的嗎？

(   ) 3 ｜ a 不用搬椅子，我可以站著吃。

         b 不用搬椅子，我可以用站的吃。

(   ) 4 ｜ a 明天放假，我們來去公園烤肉。

         b 明天不上班，咱們到公園去烤肉。

(   ) 5 ｜ a 這支手機是有特別需要的時候在用的，不是給你打遊戲用的。

         b 你有特別需要的時候才能用這支手機，可別拿它來打遊戲。

II. 填空
Fill in the blank:

> a 在 ｜ b 來去 ｜ c 用

1 ｜ A：我最近常常「看」＿＿＿＿念的書。

    B：你是說聽有聲書啊。

2 ｜ A：你平常有沒有＿＿＿＿跑步？哪天我們一起去跑步？

    B：睡覺都來不及，哪有時間啊？

3 ｜ A：今天有誰要一起＿＿＿＿喝酒呢？

    B：我今天頭痛，要早點回家休息，你找阿東吧。

4 ｜ A：這種感冒藥怎麼吃啊？

    B：給小林看一下，他是＿＿＿＿賣藥的，一定知道。

5 | A： 你昨天說你的鑰匙不見了，後來是怎麼進門的？

B： _____ 爬牆的啊。

6 | A： 你現在有_____忙什麼嗎？幫我看一下電視怎麼變黑白了？

B： 我寫完數學就幫你。

▶ 挑戰你自己：用「在／來去／用」的句型繼續上面任何一個對話。

Challenge yourself: Continue any of the conversations above with the sentence pattern of zài / láiqù / yòng.

:: **情境例句 Contextual Example**   ∩ MP3-015

A：這麼晚了，你一個人走路回去
　　會不會危險啊？

B：不會啦，別擔心，我一到家就
　　給你打電話。

A：It's so late. Will it be dangerous for
　　you to walk back alone?

B：No, don't worry, I will call you as
　　soon as I get home.

:: **句型 Sentence Pattern**

1 | Sub ＋（不）會＋ V$_{st}$。
2 | Sub ＋會不會／怎麼會＋ V$_{st}$？

普通話句型 Compare with Pǔtōnghuà
Sub ＋（不）＋ V$_{st}$

中 我這麼穿很奇怪嗎？　　Is it weird for me to dress this way?
台 你這樣穿會很奇怪。　　It's weird for you to dress this way.

:: **用法 Usage**

　　「會」在這組句型中是助詞，放在主語的後面，表示一件事的可能性或者
某種傾向。

　　In this set of patterns, "huì" is an auxiliary verb that is placed after the subject to
indicate a possibility or a certain tendency of a fact.

課本沒教的台灣華語句型50

1 | 句型 1

1.1 | 今天的客人很喜歡吃辣的菜，所以今天我做的菜都會辣。

1.2 | 這家麵包店的餅乾不會很甜。

1.3 | 你去看看冷氣是不是壞了，已經開了半個小時了還不會冷。

1 | Pattern 1

1.1 | Today's guests like spicy food, so the food I cook today is all spicy.

1.2 | The biscuits in this bakery are not very sweet.

1.3 | Go check if the air conditioner is broken. It has been running for half an hour and the room hasn't yet cooled down.

2 | 句型 2

2.1 | 小學一年級的學生每天花兩個小時做功課會不會太多了？

2.2 | 你吃這麼少怎麼會飽？

2.3 | 早上五點半起床怎麼會很早？有人起得更早呢。

2 | Pattern 2

2.1 | Wouldn't it be too much for students in first grade to spend two hours a day doing homework?

2.2 | How can you be full as you eat so little?

2.3 | How could it be early that I get up at 5:30 in the morning? Someone got up even earlier.

! 你知道嗎 Do you know

　　「會」除了表示可能性以外，還可以表示有能力做某事或者善於做某事，例如：「她會跳舞。」「他很會說故事」。台灣華語用來表示推測的可能性和某種傾向的時候，用「會」的頻率相當高。相較之下，普通話除了用「會」，還用「能」來表示，例如：「這個計畫，老闆會／能同意吧？」

　　In addition to indicating possibility, "huì" also means being able to do something or being good at doing something, e.g., "Tā huì tiàowǔ. (She can dance.)" "Tā hěn huì shuō gùshì. (He is good at telling stories.)" In Táiwān Huáyǔ, "huì" is quite frequently used to indicate a speculative possibility or a certain tendency. In contrast, "néng" plays the same function besides "huì" in Pǔtōnghuà, e.g., "Zhè ge jìhuà, lǎobǎn huì / néng tóngyì ba? (The boss will agree to this project, right?)"

NOTE

:: **情境例句 Contextual Example**　　　🎧 MP3-017

A：去美國十天玩得怎麼樣啊？

A：How did you enjoy your 10-day visit to the US?

B：十天太短了，根本沒玩到，都在坐車。

B：Ten days were too short. I didn't even have fun at all. I just sat in the car all the time.

:: **句型 Sentence Pattern**

1｜Sub ＋有／沒＋ V_{act} ＋到＋（Obj）。
2｜Sub ＋（有／沒／別）＋ V_{st} ＋到＋（了）。
3｜Sub ＋（不／沒）＋被 ＋（N）＋V ＋到。

:: **用法 Usage**

　　句型 1 的「到」意思是達成某一個動作目標。句型 2 的「到」意思是達到某一個狀態。句型 3 的動詞可以是動作動詞，也可以是狀態動詞，「到」這裡也是指達成某個動作目標或是達到某一個狀態，「被」後面的名詞是使主語受到影響的來源，但不一定需要出現。

"dào" means to achieve a certain action goal in Pattern 1, and it means to reach a certain state in Pattern 2. In Pattern 3, the verb can be either active or stative, and "dào" here also means to achieve the goal of an action or to reach a certain state. The noun following "bèi" is the source of the subject being affected, but it is optional.

:: **例句 Example**　　　🎧 MP3-018

1｜**句型 1**

1.1｜大家都在搶著買衛生紙，好像有買到才安心。

1｜**Pattern 1**

1.1｜Everyone is rushing to buy toilet paper. It seems that the mind can only be eased after getting it.

1.2 | 我還沒跟他說到話，他就走了。

1.2 | Before I could speak to him, he left.

1.3 | 這真的是西瓜汁嗎？我完全沒喝到西瓜的味道啊。

1.3 | Is this really watermelon juice? I didn't taste any watermelon flavor at all.

2 | 句型 2

2 | Pattern 2

2.1 | 山上天氣冷，多帶一點衣服，別冷到了。

2.1 | It's cold on the mountain. Bring more clothes and don't get cold.

2.2 | 我週末打掃家裡，從一樓到三樓，真的有累到。

2.2 | I cleaned the house on the weekend, from the first floor to the third floor, and I was really tired.

2.3 | 新工作有沒有讓你忙到？有時間出來玩嗎？

2.3 | Does your new job keep you busy? Do you have time to come out to play?

3 | 句型 3

3 | Pattern 3

3.1 | 妹妹昨天被弟弟氣到，今天妹妹還不跟弟弟說話。

3.1 | My younger sister was so angry with my younger brother yesterday. Today she is still not talking to him.

3.2 | 最近壞消息特別多，大家的心情很難不被影響到。

3.2 | There has been so much bad news recently. It's hard for everyone not to be emotionally affected.

3.3 | 今天的四川菜還吃得習慣嗎？有沒有被辣到？

3.3 | How do you like the Sichuan food today? Is your tongue on fire?

！你知道嗎 Do you know

　　用「V-到」表示達成動作目標或達到某一個狀態的用法，在台灣華語和普通話中都有，「到」的後面還可以接名詞組、動詞組或子句來表示動作或者狀態達到某種程度，例如：「鞋子髒到穿不出門了，不洗一洗不行。」另外還有兩個用法也是台灣華語和普通話都有的，一個是指人或是物移動到某一個地方，例如：「我把你的藥放到袋子裡了。」另一個用法是指動作繼續到某個時間，例如：「他找到半夜還沒找到爺爺。」受到台語的影響，「V-到」在台灣華語中用得相當普遍，特別是「有 / 沒＋ V_{act} ＋到」後面不接賓語，以及「V_{st} ＋到」不接達到的狀態或程度，也就是句型 1 和句型 2，但這兩者是很少見於普通話的。

    "V-dào" is used in both Táiwān Huáyǔ and Pǔtōnghuà to indicate the achievement of an action or the attainment of a state. "dào" can be followed by a noun, verb, or clause to indicate that the action or state has reached a certain level, e.g., "Xiézi zāng dào chuān bù chū mén le, bù xǐ yì xǐ bù xíng. (The shoes are so dirty that I can't wear them without washing them.)" The pattern has two other usages in both Táiwān Huáyǔ and Pǔtōnghuà. One refers to the movement of a person or object to a certain place, e.g., "Wǒ bǎ nǐ de yào fàng dào dàizi lǐ le. (I put your medicine in the bag.)" Another usage is to continue the action until a certain time, e.g., "Tā zhǎo dào bàn yè hái méi zhǎo dào yéye. (He hasn't found his grandfather by midnight.)" Influenced by Taiwanese, the usage "V-dào" is quite common in Táiwān Huáyǔ, especially when "yǒu / méi + V_{act} + dào" is not followed by an object, and "V_{st} + dào" is not followed by the degree of status reached, i.e., Pattern 1 and Pattern 2. Both of the usages, however, are rarely seen in Pǔtōnghuà.

NOTE

V ＋ 起來 qǐlái sentence

:: **情境例句 Contextual Example** 🎧 MP3-019

A：哇，好漂亮的蛋糕啊！

B：等一下！我拍起來放到網上你
再吃。

A： Wow, what a beautiful cake!

B： Wait! Let me take a picture and post
it online before you eat it.

:: **句型 Sentence Pattern**

1｜V ＋（得／不）＋起來
2｜把＋ Obj ＋ V$_{act}$ ＋起來
3｜V$_{act}$ ＋起來＋放

:: **用法 Usage**

　　這一組句型中的「起來」意思是指完成某一件事或是達到一定的目的、結
果，並且成果是可以存留的。句型 1 的動詞可以是動作動詞，也可以是狀態動詞。
句型 2 的動詞只能是動作動詞。句型 3 也只能是動作動詞，是指藉由某個動作，
預先儲備某些東西。

　　The word "qǐlái" in this set of patterns means to accomplish something or to achieve
a certain purpose or result, and the result can be retained. The verb in Pattern 1 can be
either an action verb or a stative verb. The verb in Pattern 2 can only be an action verb.
The verb in Pattern 3 is also an action verb, which means that something is stored in
advance by an action.

:: **例句 Example** 🎧 MP3-020

1｜**句型 1**

1.1｜我來教你怎麼跟老闆說話，你
可以學起來。

1.2｜他的狗受傷了，好幾天不吃東
西，這樣好得起來嗎？

1｜**Pattern 1**

1.1｜ Let me teach you how to talk to your
boss. You may learn it.

1.2｜ His dog is injured and hasn't eaten
for several days. Will he get well like
this?

1.3 | 去旅行要準備的東西太多了，我記不起來，你再說一次啦。

1.3 | There are so many things to prepare for the trip. I can't remember. Please say it again.

2 | 句型 2

2.1 | 你把我的電話號碼寫起來，有需要的時候就打給我。

2.2 | 把餃子做起來，什麼時候想吃就有得吃。

2 | Pattern 2

2.1 | Write down my phone number. Call me when you need.

2.2 | Make dumplings. Whenever you want to eat, you can have them.

3 | 句型 3

3.1 | 她很喜歡喝咖啡，一看到特別的就會買起來放，所以家裡總有喝不完的咖啡。

3.2 | 晚餐我已經煮起來放了，你餓了就自己吃吧，我先出門了。

3.3 | 天氣變熱了，可以把冬天的衣服收起來放了。

3 | Pattern 3

3.1 | She likes to drink coffee very much. She buys it whenever she sees a special blend, so there is always an endless supply of coffee at home.

3.2 | I have already cooked dinner. If you are hungry, help yourself. I am taking off now.

3.3 | The weather is getting hot. You can put away your winter clothes now.

❗ 你知道嗎 Do you know

「V-起來」的「起來」在中文裡一共有六種用法：

第一種是表示人或者事物以某個動作或姿態由下向上在空間中的移動，例如「站／拿／搬／跳起來」，例句：「要唱國歌了，大家請站起來」。

第二種是表示某物向一個目標移動或聚集，例如「連／圍／收集起來」，例句：「火車是一節一節連起來的。」

第三種是表示某個動作或事物的發生開始並繼續下去，例如「轉／動／流行起來」，例句：「台灣的珍珠奶茶這幾年在日本流行起來了。」

第四種是表示某一種狀態開始發展，並且程度繼續加深，搭配的是狀態動詞，例如「緊張／開心／生氣起來」。例句：「比賽還沒開始，我就緊張起來了。」

第五種是表示以某種感官或動作的方式來評價某事，例如「看／聽／吃起來」，例句：「看起來明天會下雨。」

　　最後一種就是前面的句型介紹的，指的是某一個動作的完成或是達到一定的目的、結果。這個用法無論是台灣華語還是普通話都有，但這個用法在台灣可以搭配的動詞比普通話多。普通話一般搭配兩類動詞，一是「掛、排、搭、擺」等有鋪陳意思的，二是「關、蓋、裝、收、保存」等有封存意思的，但台灣華語不限於這兩類的動詞。

In Mandarin Chinese, there are six ways to use the word "qǐlái" in "V qǐlái."

　　The first one is to express that a person or a thing is performing a certain action or motion in space from the bottom up, e.g., "zhàn 'stand' / ná 'take' / bān 'move' / tiào 'jump' qǐlái", e.g., "Yào chàng guógē le, dàjiā qǐng zhàn qǐlái. (It's time to sing the national anthem. Everyone, please stand up.)"

　　The second way is to indicate that something is moving or gathering towards a goal, e.g., "lián 'connect' / wéi 'enclose' / shōují 'collect' qǐlái", e.g., "Huǒchē shì yì jié yì jié lián qǐlái de. (The train is connected by carts one after another.)"

　　The third way is to indicate the beginning of an action or something that happens and continues, e.g., "zhuǎn 'turn' /dòng 'move' / liúxíng 'popularize' qǐlái", e.g., "Táiwān de zhēnzhūnǎichá zhè jǐ nián zài Rìběn liúxíng qǐlái le. (Taiwan's boba milk tea has become popular in Japan in the past few years.)"

　　The fourth way is to indicate that a certain state is beginning to develop and the degree continuing to deepen, with a stative verb, such as "jǐnzhāng 'nervous' / kāixīn 'happy' / shēngqì 'mad' qǐlái." e.g., "Bǐsài hái méi kāishǐ, wǒ jiù jǐnzhāng qǐlái le. (I'm getting nervous even before the game starts.)"

　　The fifth way is to evaluate something in a sensory or motor way, such as kàn 'look' / tīng 'listen' / chī 'eat' qǐlái, e.g., "Kàn qǐlái míngtiān huì xiàyǔ. (It looks like it will rain tomorrow.)"

　　The last way is the way introduced in the listed patterns above, which refers to the completion of an action or the achievement of a certain purpose or result. The usage is common in both Táiwān Huáyǔ and Pǔtōnghuà, but the collocated verbs in Táiwān Huáyǔ are more than in Pǔtōnghuà. In Pǔtōnghuà, there are only two types of collocated verbs: those that mean displaying, such as guà 'hang', pái 'arrange', dā 'build', bǎi 'lay', and those that mean containing, such as guān 'close', gài 'cover', zhuāng 'pack', shōu 'put away', bǎocún 'save', but the collocated verbs are not limited to these two types in Táiwān Huáyǔ.

NOTE

10 | V_{act} + 看看 kànkan sentence

:: 情境例句 Contextual Example 🎧 MP3-021

A：這雙鞋大小合適嗎？起來走看看。

B：有點緊。拿大半號的來試看看好了。

A：Are the shoes the right size? Get up and try to walk around.

B：A bit tight. Let me try a half size bigger.

:: 句型 Sentence Pattern

1 | V_{act} ＋ 看看
2 | V_{act} ＋ Obj ＋ 看看
3 | V_{act} ＋ 看看 ＋ Obj

普通話句型 Compare with Pǔtōnghuà
∨∨看

中 你想想看，怎麼可能有人不喜歡跟我做朋友？
Think about it, how could someone not like to be friends with me?

台 你想看看，為什麼大家都不喜歡跟你做朋友？
Think about it, how could everyone not like to be friends with you?

:: 用法 Usage

　　這組句型裡的動詞可以是單音節，也可以是雙音節，表示試著做某個動作。常常用在建議別人或者請求別人做某一件事的時候，而且不可以用在已經發生的事情。句型 2 的賓語一般是音節比較短的詞。句型 3 的賓語可以是比較長的，甚至可以是一個子句。

　　The verbs in these patterns are either monosyllabic or disyllabic, indicating an attempt to do an action or something. It is often used when giving a suggestion or making a request, and cannot be used in the context of something that has already happened. In Pattern 2, the object is generally a word with a shorter syllable, whereas the object in Pattern 3 can be longer or even a clause.

:: **例句 Example**

MP3-022

1 | 句型 1

1.1 | 我做了一個蛋糕,請大家吃看看。

1.2 | 這首歌是這樣唱的……你們練習看看。

1 | Pattern 1

1.1 | I made a cake. Please try it.

1.2 | This song is sung like this... You guys try to practice.

2 | 句型 2

2.1 | 這個問題我也不會,去問老師看看吧。

2.2 | 不知道這湯夠不夠鹹,我來喝一口看看。

2.3 | 第二外語你可以選日語看看,日語老師教得很好。

2 | Pattern 2

2.1 | I don't know this question either. Go ask the teacher.

2.2 | I don't know if this soup is salty enough. Let me try a sip.

2.3 | You can choose Japanese as a second foreign language. The Japanese teacher is very good at what he does.

3 | 句型 3

3.1 | 聽說你們的新辦公室很漂亮,我想參觀看看你們的新辦公室。

3.2 | 這個計畫不錯,你注意看看有沒有什麼公司能接這個計畫。

3.3 | 你們討論看看明年公司旅遊要去什麼地方。

3 | Pattern 3

3.1 | I heard that your new office is very beautiful. I would like to visit your new office.

3.2 | This project is not bad. You should be on the lookout to see if there is any company that can take it on.

3.3 | You try to discuss where to go for the company trip next year.

　　在台灣也用「VV 看」來表達嘗試做某個動作，但是後面不接賓語或子句，動作對象的賓語一般已經在前面提到了。普通話也有「VV 看」這個用法。但是必須是像「吃、看、喝、聽」等單音節的動詞才能用在「VV 看」的句型。如果是雙音節的動詞需要以「ABAB」的形式來表現嘗試的語義，例如「練習練習、討論討論、檢查檢查」。

　　In Táiwān Huáyǔ, "VV kàn" is also used to express an attempt to do a certain action, but it is not followed by a phrase or clause, and the object of the action is usually already mentioned in the preceding sentence. Such usage also exists in Pǔtōnghuà. However, only monosyllabic verbs, such as chī 'eat', kàn 'see', hē 'drink' and tīng 'listen', can be used in "VV kàn" pattern. If it is a disyllabic verb. It should be in the form of "ABAB" to show the semantic meaning of attempt, such as liànxí liànxí 'practice', tǎolùn tǎolùn 'discuss', jiǎnchá jiǎnchá 'check'.

NOTE

I. 用（）裡的詞把句子變換成台灣華語的表達方式：

Use the words in ( ) to transform the sentences into expressions of Táiwān Huáyǔ:

例 餅乾原來是這樣做啊，那我練習練習。（看）

→ 餅乾原來是這樣做啊，那我練習看看。

1 | 最近報告很多，今天老師一進教室就給我們考試，還好我昨天晚上讀了書。（到）

_____

2 | 你看這個東西掛在那兒是不是太高了？（會）

_____

3 | 對電腦的麻煩我很有經驗，你電腦的問題我可以檢查檢查。（看）

_____

4 | 我開了半個小時，這門還是開不了（liǎo）！（起來）

_____

5 | 跑了十公里，現在真的餓了。（到）

_____

6 | 那麼多漢堡、飲料用這個袋子裝得下嗎？（起來）

_____

II. 填空

Fill in the blank:

a 看看　｜　b 會　｜　c 不會　｜　d 到　｜　e 起來

1 | A：要怎麼做才可以像你一樣拍出這麼美的照片呢？

　　B：第一件事當然是把錢準備 _____，買一台好相機啊。

2｜A：阿明來了嗎？再不走要遲到了。

　　B：還沒呢，你們先去吧，我再等 _____ 。

3｜A：你別七月去台灣，七月 _____ 很熱。

　　B：可是我只有七月能放長假，熱就熱吧。

4｜A：你幫我看一下我買這個健康保險有沒有被貴 _____ ？

　　B：我看看……

5｜A：你認識李經理嗎？我想找他談生意。

　　B：認識啊，他剛出國回來，不知道最近忙不忙。我幫你約他 _____ 。

6｜A：晚上的客人有五個，我們家的筷子、湯匙夠嗎？

　　B：我已經都先洗 _____ 放了，沒問題的。

7｜A：你覺得這種咖啡怎麼樣？

　　B：很好喝， _____ 很苦。

> ▶ 挑戰你自己：用「看看／會／到／起來」的句型繼續上面任何
> 一個對話。
>
> Challenge yourself: Continue any of the above conversations with the
> sentence pattern of V-kànkan / huì /dào / qǐlái.

語氣助詞

　　語氣詞沒有特定的意義，但卻是句子的調味料，給予言談各種風味。想像一下上課的時候學生不專心，A 老師說：「看這裡！」，B 老師說：「看這裡喔！」讓人感覺 A 老師很兇，而 B 老師溫柔得多。這是因為「喔」帶有提醒的意味，使得命令的語氣和緩得多，讓 B 老師的態度顯得比較友善。在口語中用不用語氣詞，可以顯示說話者的情緒或者態度，同時也可以表露跟對話另一方的關係是不是親近的，或者雙方有沒有地位高低差別。在和別人溝通的時候，使用語氣詞往往能夠調節人際關係，但是在會議、報告、演講等正式場合應該避免使用。許多人注意到所謂的「台灣腔」就是語氣詞使用得特別多，可以說是台灣人說話的特色之一。這裡所介紹的是在普通話中比較少見的台灣華語語氣詞。另外，有些語氣詞可以當作感嘆詞，單獨出現或放在句首，這些用法都會在這個單元中說明。

Modal Particles

Modal particles have no specific meaning, but they act as spices for sentences and give speeches a variety of flavors. Imagine this situation: When students are distracted in class, Teacher A says: "kàn zhèlǐ! (Look here!)", and Teacher B says: "kàn zhèlǐ ō!" People would get the impression that Teacher A is severe, while Teacher B is much gentler. It is the particle "ō" that softens the tone in a command. That is why Teacher B seems more friendly. Using of modal particles or not can indicate the moods and attitudes of the speaker, as well as whether the relationship between the speaker and the interlocutor is close. It can also indicate the power status between them. When communicating with others, the use of modal particles can often regulate interpersonal relationships, but you should avoid using them in formal settings such as meetings, presentations, and speeches. Many people have noticed that the so-called "Taiwanese accent" has a particularly frequent and diverse usage of modal particles. This is one of the characteristics of Taiwanese speech. The Táiwān Huáyǔ modal particles introduced here in Part II are rare in Pǔtōnghuà. In addition, some modal particles can be used as interjections, either on their own or at the beginning of a sentence. They will be explained in this part as well.

11 喔 ō

:: **情境例句 Contextual Example**　　🎧 MP3-024

A： 過馬路要小心喔！
B： 嗯，知道了。

A： Be careful crossing the street!
B： Ok, got it.

:: **句型 Sentence Pattern**

1｜S ＋喔
2｜Sub ＋好＋ V_{st} ＋喔！
3｜是喔。／真的喔。
4｜喔（感嘆詞）

:: **用法 Usage**

　　語氣詞「喔」有高音和低音的用法，句型 1 如果是祈使句和陳述句用的是高音，表示說話者的提醒或是想引起注意，帶有說話者對聽話者關愛的意味。如果是疑問句用的是低音，帶有說話者不確定或者試探的意味。句型 2 是感嘆句，用的也是低音，表示說話者深刻的主觀評價或感受。句型 3 是在跟別人交談的時候回應別人的話，表示自己認真地在聽對方說話，用的也是低音。句型 4 的「喔」用在句首做為感嘆詞，如果語調是上揚的，表示驚訝，意思是「真的嗎？」如果是語調下降的、低音的,意思是「明白了。」如果「喔」的音發得很長，意思是說話者終於理解明白了。

　　"ō" can be used in high pitch or low pitch. In Pattern 1, high "ō" is used if the sentence is an imperative sentence or a statement. The function is to remind or draw attention to the speaker's concern or care for the listener. If the sentence is a question, "ō" is in low pitch. It implies the speaker's uncertainty or probing. Pattern 2 is an exclamatory sentence and "ō" is also in low pitch to express the speaker's subjective evaluation or feelings. Pattern 3 is used in a conversation to respond to the interlocutor to show that he or she is listening to the interlocutor. "ō" here is in low pitch as well. "ō" in Pattern 4 is used as an interjection at the beginning of a sentence. If the intonation is rising, it means "really?" If the intonation is falling and in low pitch, it means "I got it." If "ō" is prolonged, it implies that the speaker finally realizes what the interlocutor is saying.

:: **例句 Example**　　　　　　　　🎧 MP3-025

1 | **句型 1**

1.1 | A：電腦修好了，你檢查一下喔。

　　 B：好的，謝謝你。

1.2 | A：他女朋友很漂亮喔，眼睛大大的，圓圓的。

　　 B：是喔，你見過喔。

1.3 | A：你星期天要出去玩！？星期一要交的報告寫完了喔？

　　 B：早就寫完了。

2 | **句型 2**

2.1 | A：這菜好辣喔！快給我水！

　　 B：來，這杯拿去喝。

2.2 | A：這隻狗好可愛喔，叫什麼名字呢？

　　 B：牠叫小白。

3 | **句型 3**

3.1 | A：我現在在減肥，不吃晚飯。

　　 B：是喔，這樣不會餓得受不

1 | **Pattern 1**

1.1 | A：The computer is fixed, please have a look.

1.2 | B：OK. Thank you.

　　 A：His girlfriend is very pretty, with big and round eyes.

　　 B：Really? You have seen her?

1.3 | A：You're going out to play on Sunday!? You finished the report that you need to turn in on Monday?

　　 B：It's long done.

2 | **Pattern 2**

2.1 | A：This food is so spicy! Give me water quickly!

　　 B：Here. Take this glass.

2.2 | A：This dog is so cute. What's his name?

　　 B：His name is Xiao Bai.

3 | **Pattern 3**

3.1 | A：I am on a diet now. I don't eat dinner.

　　 B：Is that so? Aren't you too hungry for that?

3.2 | A：我以前住在十四樓，有一次電梯壞了一個星期，每天都要爬樓梯，累死了。

B：真的喔，怎麼會壞那麼久？

4 | 句型 4

4.1 | A：小姐，我們沒有點這個菜，你送錯了。

B：喔？對不起，我去查一下。

4.2 | A：下次注意，不要再打翻杯子了。

B：喔，我會小心一點的。

4.3 | A：這個盒子要從這裡才打得開。

B：喔，這樣啊，我開了半天都開不起來。

3.2 | A：I used to live on the fourteenth floor. Once the elevator was broken for a week. I had to climb the stairs every day. I was exhausted.

B：Really, how could it be broken for so long?

4 | Pattern 4

4.1 | A：Miss, we didn't order this dish, wrong table.

B：Oh? Sorry, I'll go check.

4.2 | A：Next time, pay attention and don't knock over the glass again.

B：Ok. I'll be more careful.

4.3 | A：This box can only be opened from here.

B：Oh, that's why! I haven't been able to open it for a long time.

❗ 原來如此 No Wonder

「喔」是台灣華語中相當高頻的語氣詞。一般來說，女性用得比男性多，特別是母親對小孩子說話的時候，在要求孩子言行的語句也經常加上「喔」來緩和語氣。現在因為海峽兩岸的交流越來越密切，普通話使用語氣詞「喔」的頻率也有逐漸增加的趨勢，但普通話常寫做「哦」，有的時候也寫做「喔」或「噢」。台灣華語把「哦」用在句首當感嘆詞，和句型 4 的用法一樣，說的時候拉長下降的語調，意思是說話者終於理解明白了。

"ō" is a frequently-used modal particle in Táiwān Huáyǔ. It is generally used by females more than males, especially by mothers when they speak to their children to soften the tone of commands and warnings. As cross-strait exchanges become more and more common, the use of the particle "ō" in Pǔtōnghuà is gradually increasing. However, the character is written as " 哦 ", or sometimes as " 喔 " or " 噢 ", to represent the modal particle. " 哦 " is used in the beginning of a sentence as an interjection, like in Pattern 4, with a prolonged falling intonation in Táiwān Huáyǔ. It conveys the sense that the speaker finally realizes something.

12 耶 ye

:: **情境例句 Contextual Example** 🎧 MP3-026

A：你今天穿得很漂亮耶！有約會嗎？

B：什麼話嘛，沒有約會就不能穿得漂亮一點嗎？

A： You look beautiful today! Do you have a date?

B： What are you talking about? Can't I wear something nice without a date?

:: **句型 Sentence Pattern**

1 | S ＋耶

:: **用法 Usage**

　　「耶」用在陳述句尾表示說話者想歡呼或是覺得興奮、驚訝、氣憤或讚嘆的時候，帶有要把自己強烈的情緒分享給別人的意味。

"ye" is used at the end of a statement when the speaker wants to cheer or feels excited, surprised, anger, or admiration. It implies that the speaker wants to share his or her strong emotions with others.

:: **例句 Example** 🎧 MP3-027

1 | **興奮**

A：我終於買到演唱會的票了耶！！

B：真好，我都買不到。

1 | **Excitement**

A： I finally got tickets to the concert. Yay!!

B： So nice, I couldn't even get one.

2 | **驚訝**

A：你今天沒戴眼鏡耶！這樣看得到嗎？

B：沒關係，你是我的眼睛。

2 | **Surprise**

A： You aren't wearing glasses today! Can you see things like this?

B： That's fine. You are my eyes.

73

3 | 氣憤

A：這個蛋糕是我買的耶！你怎麼一點都沒留，全部都吃完了？

B：對不起，我再買一個還你。

3 | Anger

A：I bought this cake! Why did you eat it all and not leave me a piece?

B：I'm sorry, I'll buy you another one.

4 | 讚嘆

A：你不認識阿星？他很棒耶！游泳拿了全國第一名。

B：不認識。

4 | Admiration

A：You don't know A Xing? He is awesome! He won first place in the nationwide swimming competition.

B：I don't know him.

！你知道嗎 Do you know

　　歡呼用的語氣詞「耶」與英語「yay」的作用一樣，都是說話者因為興奮呼喊出來，並且希望別人也可以受到感染。「耶」還用在其他濃烈的情緒上，如上面的例句所示範的。在社交媒體中，因為講求人與人之間的分享，可以發現「耶」是使用頻率相當高的語氣詞。其實在古代漢語中「耶」是疑問助詞，相當於現在的「嗎」和「呢」，「是耶？非耶？」意思就是「是嗎？不是嗎？」。

　　The function of "ye" for cheering is the same as English "yay." The speaker shouts out in excitement and hopes others can share the excitement. "ye" is also used to express other strong emotions as mentioned in the examples above. The word "ye" can be found quite frequently on social media when sharing news or moods with others, as sharing is the key feature of social media. However, in classical Chinese, "ye" was an interrogative particle, equivalent to "mā" and "ne" today. The sentence "shì yé? fēi yé?" means "is it? isn't it?"

13   說 shuō

:: **情境例句 Contextual Example**   MP3-028

A：我回來了！

B：太棒了，你回來了，好久沒見
到你了說。

A：I'm back!

B：Wonderful, you are back. It has been
so long since I last saw you.

:: **句型 Sentence Pattern**

1 | S ＋說

:: **用法 Usage**

　語氣詞「說」使用在說話最後一句的句末，用法有三種，一是表示說話者
的判斷；二是跟說話者的預期相反；三是給聽話者提出友善的建議或警告。

　"shuō" is used as an utterance ending. The usage of "shuō" expresses: 1) the
speaker's estimate; 2) the speaker's anticipation of being contradicted; or 3) the
speaker trying to give a suggestion or warning in a friendly tone to the interlocutor.

:: **例句 Example**   MP3-029

1 | **判斷**

A：你不能選別的時間嗎？我
星期六有事說。

B：不早說。

1 | **Estimate**

A：Can't you pick another time? I
am busy on Saturday.

B：You didn't say that earlier.

2 | **與預期相反**

A：這個西瓜不會甜說。

B：我覺得有甜啊。

2 | **Counter-anticipation**

A：This watermelon is not sweet.

B：I think it's sweet.

3 | 建議

A：我從來沒有自己做過蛋
糕，你一定要照幾張你做
的蛋糕給我們看看說。

B：沒問題，一定拍給你看。

3 | Suggestion

A : I've never made a cake myself
before. You must show us some
pictures of the cake you made.

B : No problem. I'll take a photo to
show you.

！你知道嗎 Do you know

「說」作為語氣詞的功能是從台語而來的，普通話中沒有相對應的語氣詞，並且比起日常對話，「說」這個語氣詞更常以文字的形式使用在網路或通訊軟體中，用來模擬口語語氣。在吵架或比較不愉快的情境下，使用「說」在句尾會讓語氣帶有威脅感。 比如爸爸要孩子趕快準備好出門上學，但孩子還是拖拖拉拉，爸爸就說：「快點，要不然你不要去上學說。」

"shuō" obtained the modal particle function from Taiwanese. There is no corresponding word in Pǔtōnghuà, and the modal particle is used online in written form more than it is spoken in real life to sound like talking off-line. In an argument or unpleasant situation, the use of "shuō" at the end of a sentence makes the tone threatening. For example, if a father urges his kid to get ready for school, but the child dawdles, the father may say, "Kuìdiǎn, yàobùrán nǐ bú yào qù shàng xué shuō. (Hurry up, or else don't go to school.)"

第二單元：語氣助詞

PART II: Modal Particles

14 啦 la

:: **情境例句 Contextual Example**　　　🎧 MP3-030

A：謝謝你，我吃飽了。
B：不要這麼客氣，再吃一碗啦。

A： Thank you, I'm full.
B： Don't be so polite. Have another bowl.

:: **句型 Sentence Pattern**

1 ｜ S ＋啦
2 ｜ 好啦。／對啦。
3 ｜ ……A 啦、B 啦、C 啦……

:: **用法 Usage**

　　「啦」有高音和低音兩種用法，句型 1 是低音的「啦」，可以是陳述句，也可以是疑問句，用法有三種：一是表示說話者肯定自己的所說的；二是表現說話者非常堅持的態度；三是顯露說話者不耐煩、不悅的態度。句型 2「好啦」、「對啦」是固定用法，給人不耐煩的感覺，有時候反覆說兩次來表現出說話者強烈的負面情緒。句型 3 用在列舉多個項目的情況，把高音的「啦」加在每個名詞的後面。

　　"la" can be used in high pitch or low pitch. It is low "la" in Pattern 1. The sentence is either a statement or a question. There are three ways to use the pattern: 1) the speaker affirms his or her own statement; 2) the speaker's attitude is very insistent; and 3) the speaker is impatient and unhappy. In Pattern 2, "hǎo la" and "duì la" are fixed expressions to express the speaker's strongly negative emotions with the attitude of impatience. They are sometimes repeated twice. In Pattern 3, high "la" is used after nouns when listing multiple items.

1 | 句型 1

1.1 | 肯定陳述

A：唉，我最近總是忘記帶鑰匙出門。

B：你一定是老了啦。

1.2 | 堅持的態度

（下大雨的時候，B 要給躲雨的 A 愛心傘）

A：不用了，謝謝。等一下雨就停了。

B：沒關係啦！你就帶走，不用還我。

1.3 | 不耐煩

A：跟你說這杯喝了咳嗽就好了，你喝不喝啦？

B：味道有點可怕，我不要。

2 | 句型 2

2.1 | A：大家都要去，你去不去啦？

B：好啦，好啦，我去。

2.2 | A：這種爛人，你還愛他幹嘛？

B：我也不想啊，你不懂的。

A：對啦！我不懂，你最懂！

1 | Pattern 1

1.1 | Affirmative

A：Sigh. I've been forgetting to take my keys with me lately.

B：You must be getting old.

1.2 | Insist

(When it rains heavily, B would like to give an umbrella to A, who is sheltering from the rain)

A：No, thanks. The rain will stop in a while.

B：It's okay! Just take it with you. No need to give it back to me.

1.3 | Impatient

A：I've told you that if you drink this, your cough will be gone. Would you drink it?

B：The smell is a bit horrible. I don't want it.

2 | Pattern 2

2.1 | A：Everyone's going. Are you going or not?

B：All right, all right, I'll go.

2.2 | A：Why do you still love such an asshole?

B：I don't want to, but you don't understand.

A：Right! I don't understand. You do!

第二單元：語氣助詞　PART II: Modal Particles

3 | 句型 3

3.1 | 如果你要請她看電影，她什麼電影都看，喜劇片啦、恐怖片啦、動作片啦，什麼都好。

3.2 | 昨天跑了二十一公里，現在全身酸痛，腿啦、手啦、背啦……不知道幾天才會好？

3 | Pattern 3

3.1 | If you want to invite her to a movie, she'll watch anything – comedy, horror, action, anything will be good.

3.2 | Yesterday I ran 21 kilometers. Now my whole-body aches, my legs, hands, back... don't know how many days will it take to get over?

❗ 你知道嗎 Do you know

「啦」在普通話中也用，是「了」和「啊」連音的語氣詞，這個用法台灣華語中也有。這個「啦」也有高音、低音兩種用法，高音的「啦」讓說話者拉近與對話者的距離，顯得比較友善輕鬆，比方一個男孩問他哥哥昨天的蛋糕呢？哥哥說：「吃完啦。」相對於「吃完了。」感覺起來輕鬆隨意得多，好像不是什麼大不了的事，雖然對男孩來說，這兩種回答方法的結果都是他吃不到蛋糕。低音「啦」經常用在關懷對話方的時候，比方同事猜想你為什麼今天上班遲到而說：「睡晚啦？」加上「啦」就透露出期盼對方給予回應的態度。

"la" is also commonly used in Pǔtōnghuà. It is the combination of "le" and "a", and this usage exists in Táiwān Huáyǔ too. This "la" also can be in high pitch or low pitch. By using high "la", the speaker gets closer to the interlocutor figuratively and appears to be more friendly and more relaxed. For example, a boy asks his older brother where yesterday's cake is. The brother might say, "Chī wán la (It's gone)." as opposed to "Chī wán le." The former feels much more relaxed and casual, like it's not a big deal, even though both responses resulted in the boy not having cake. Low "la" is often used when a speaker is caring for the interlocutor. For example, if a co-worker wonders why you're late for work today, she / he may say, "Shuì wǎn la? (Did you sleep in?)" The word "la" is added to reveal the expectation of a response from the other side.

<u>NOTE</u>

I. 填空：根據對話，選擇一個最適當的語氣詞。

Fill in the blanks: According to the dialogue, choose the most appropriate modal particle.

a 說 ｜ b 耶 ｜ c 啦 ｜ d 喔

1｜A：奇怪，我打了五次電話給阿明，他都沒接。

　　B：你不要想太多 _____，他可能在開會，等一下就打給你了。

2｜A：小感冒，不用吃藥。記得多休息多喝水 _____。一個星期以後就會好了。

　　B：好的，謝謝醫生。

3｜A：今天公司說我們可以一個星期在家上班兩天 _____！

　　B：你真的覺得這是讓人開心的事嗎？

4｜A：你把我的照相機丟到哪裡去了 _____！我已經找了半個小時還沒找到。

　　B：不要生氣嘛，不是在你的房間嗎？

5｜A：熱死了，快把冷氣打開。

　　B：你太怕熱了吧？我們家都是三十度才開冷氣的，現在才二十九度 _____。

II. 選出適合的交談對話內容：

Choose the appropriate conversation content:

（　）1｜A：我找到新工作了！

　　　　B：❶我以為你還要念研究所說。

　　　　　❷學生如果要找工作可以去咖啡廳啦、便利商店啦、圖書館啦，都很不錯。

（　　）2｜A：最近小寶經常很晚才回來，他是在忙什麼？

B：❶小寶去上班了耶，你晚一點再來找他吧。

❷他幾歲了？還要九點以前上床睡覺喔？

（　　）3｜A：好緊張喔，比賽還剩三分鐘，還是 3：3。

B：❶爸去哪裡了？比賽快開始了說。

❷英國隊有好幾個職業選手耶，一定會贏的。

（　　）4｜A：她那麼早結婚，一定是有了。

B：❶沒有啦，你想太多了。

❷現在的人越生越少，需要多生一點說。

▶ 挑戰你自己：用語氣詞「喔／耶／說／啦」延伸上面任何一個對話。

Challenge yourself: Use modal particle ō / ye / shuō / la to extend any of the dialogues above.

15 咧 lie

:: **情境例句 Contextual Example**　　🎧 MP3-033

A：我明天就走了。　　　　　　　A： I'm leaving tomorrow.
B：那你打算什麼時候回來咧？　　B： When do you plan to come back?

:: **句型 Sentence Pattern**

1 | S ＋ 咧
2 | N ＋ 咧？
3 | S，N ＋ 咧，VP

:: **用法 Usage**

　　「咧」的使用暗示著某些訊息的對比，如情境例句中 A 說明天要走，也就是說他要離開了，然後 B 問「什麼時候回來」，加上「咧」來提示「離開」和「回來」的對比。「咧」有高音和低音兩種用法，高音「咧」用在句型 1 的問句，包括一般問句、反問句，句型 2 的省略問句，以及句型 3 中名詞的後面。如果句型 1 是陳述句，用的是低音「咧」，作用是在以下三種情況下凸顯訊息的對比：1）表示說話者要告訴聽話者有一個他可能忽略的事情；2）說話者要提出一個和聽話者預期不一樣的事情；3）說話者想要反駁對方的意見。

　　The use of the particle "lie" implies a contrast between certain messages. In the example above, A said "I'm leaving tomorrow." B responded: "When will you come back?" "Coming back" makes a contrast with "leaving." "lie" is used with either in high or low pitch. High "lie" is used at the end of questions in Pattern 1, including general questions and rhetorical questions, and elliptical questions in Pattern 2 and after the noun in Pattern 3. If it is a statement in Pattern 1, "lie" is in low pitch, and it marks the contrast between the messages delivered in the following situations: 1) the speaker is telling the listener something he or she may have overlooked; 2) the speaker is suggesting something different from what the listener expects; and 3) the speaker is trying to contradict the interlocutor.

1 | 句型 1

1.1 | 一般疑問

A：十二點了還睡不著，可以去做什麼咧？

B：就起來吃東西啊。

1.2 | 反問問句

A：暑假你不會出國去玩吧？

B：如果有錢，我怎麼會不想去咧？

1.3 | 聽話者有所忽略

A：喂～～開門啊！

B：妳叫得這麼大聲，聽不到才有鬼咧。

1.4 | 與聽者預期相反

A：你爸晚上在家吧？叫他打電話給我。

B：他要去加班咧。

1.5 | 反駁

A：我真不知道你們這些男人到底怎麼想的。

B：我才不知道你們女人在想什麼咧！

2 | 句型 2

2.1 | A：我的手機咧？

B：在這裡啊。

2.2 | A：你的漢堡咧？

B：被小林吃掉了。

1 | Pattern 1

1.1 | General question

A：It's twelve o'clock, and I still can't sleep. What can I do?

B：Just get up and eat.

1.2 | Rhetorical question

A：You're not going to go abroad for the summer vacation, are you?

B：If I had the money, why wouldn't I want to go?

1.3 | Something overlooked

A：Hey! Open the door!

B：You're shouting so loudly. How can anyone not hear you?

1.4 | Counter-expectation

A：Your father is home this evening, right? Tell him to call me.

B：He has to work overtime.

1.5 | Disagreement

A：I really don't know what you men are thinking.

B：I don't know what you women are thinking!

2 | Pattern 2

2.1 | A：Where's my phone?

B：Here it is.

2.2 | A：Where is your hamburger?

B：It was eaten by Xiao Lin.

3 | 句型 3

3.1 | 我們明天搬家，男生十點來我家；女生咧，下午兩點過來就可以了。

3.2 | 這一箱放客廳；那一箱咧，放廚房。

3 | Pattern 3

3.1 | We are going to move tomorrow. The boys need to come to my house at 10:00 a.m. As for the girls, it will be fine if you come by 2 p.m.

3.2 | This box goes to the living room. As for that box, it goes to the kitchen.

! 你知道嗎 Do you know

「咧」的用法跟「呢」幾乎一樣，兩者都有高低音的用法，也都不能用在祈使句。唯一的不同是陳述句末使用「咧」，在回應請求的情況下，讓說話者有對自己說出的話感到不好意思或帶有向對方道歉的語氣，而這個情況是不能用「呢」的。比方說朋友問你：「麻婆豆腐怎麼做啊？」，你說：「不曉得咧。」意思是你以為我知道怎麼做，我很願意告訴你，只是我也不知道怎麼做。「咧」還有另一個語音變體「捏／餒 (nei)」，語氣上比「咧」更和緩。

The usage of "lie" is almost the same as "ne." Both have usages with high pitch and low pitch, and neither can be used in an imperative sentence. The only difference is that the use of the word "lie" at the end of a statement gives the speaker a tone of embarrassment or apology for what he or she has said, in which case the word "ne" cannot be used. Let's say a friend asks you, "Mápódòufǔ zěnme zuò? (How do you make Mapo tofu?)" You said, "Bù xiǎodé lie. (I don't know.)" meaning you thought I knew how to make Mapo tofu, and I'd love to tell you, but I am sorry that I don't know how to make it either. There is another variation of "lie", "nei", which makes the speaking tone milder than using "lie."

NOTE

16 咩 mie

:: 情境例句 Contextual Example　　🎧 MP3-035

A：你怎麼還在用不能上網的手機啊？

B：就沒有需要咩。反正在家、在辦公室都可以上網。

A：Why are you still using a phone that doesn't have internet access?

B：There is no need for that. I can access the internet at home and at the office anyway.

:: 句型 Sentence Pattern

1｜S ＋咩

:: 用法 Usage

「咩」用在陳述句尾來表示說話者聲明自己的看法，無論別人是不是贊同。因為是說話者自己的看法，所以主語如果是「我」往往省略不說，句子中也經常和「就」或「就是」一起使用，來加強肯定的語氣。

"mie" is used at the end of a statement to indicate that the speaker asserts his or her own opinion, whether others agree with it or not. Because the statement is the opinion of the speaker, the subject is often omitted if it is "I." "jiù" or "jiùshì" is often used in the sentence to enhance the affirmative tone.

:: 例句 Example　　🎧 MP3-036

1｜A：出國就是吃東西、買東西咩。

B：我不覺得。我就只喜歡拍照。

1｜A：Going abroad means eating and shopping.

B：I don't think so. I just like taking photos.

2｜A：你怎麼連這個都不會？

B：就第一次用咩。

2｜A：How can you not know how to do this?

B：It's just the first time I'm using it.

課本沒教的台灣華語句型50

「咩」的用法與另一個很常用的低音語氣詞「嘛」相當接近，這個語氣詞普通話也用。「嘛」也是附在陳述句末，表示事情就該這樣、理由很明顯，暗示聽話者應該認同，例如：「有意見就說嘛，你怎麼不說呢？」。無論是「咩」還是「嘛」，如果用得太多、太過頻繁，容易讓人有自大、驕傲的印象。「嘛」還有另外一種用法是放在句子的主語或分句後，作為停頓來引起聽話者注意接下去要說的內容，例如：「小孩嘛，吵吵鬧鬧是難免的。」、「他喜歡團隊運動像是棒球、籃球，理由嘛，是可以跟很多人一起玩。」

The usage of "mie" is similar to another common modal particle, "ma" in low pitch. "ma" is also used at the end of a statement to indicate that's the way it should be because the reason is obvious and implies that the listener should agree. This usage exists in Pǔtōnghuà too. For example, "Yǒu yìjiàn jiùs shuō ma, nǐ zěnme bù shuō ne? (If you have an opinion, just say it. Why don't you say it?)" If you use either "mie" or "ma (in low pitch)" a lot or too often, it easily gives people the impression of arrogance and proud. "ma" is also used after a subject or a clause to serve as a pause in a sentence to draw the listener's attention to what is going to be said, e.g., "Xiǎohái ma, chǎochǎonàonào shì nánmiǎn de. (It is inevitable that kids are noisy.)", "Tā xǐhuān tuánduì yùndòng, xiàng shì bàngqiú, lánqiú, lǐyóu ma, shì kěyǐ gēn hěn duō rén yìqǐ wán. (He likes team sports, such as baseball and basketball. The reason is that he can play with many people.)"

第二單元：語氣助詞

PART II: Modal Particles

17 欸 eh

:: **情境例句 Contextual Example**　🎧 MP3-037

A：那家新開的咖啡店今天有買一送一欸！

B：真的嗎？那我要去買。

A：That new coffee shop is offering buy one get one free today!

B：Really? Then I'm going to buy it.

:: **句型 Sentence Pattern**

1 ｜ S ＋欸
2 ｜ 欸（感嘆詞）

:: **用法 Usage**

　　句型 1「欸」用在陳述句尾，意味說話者要說一件聽話者不知道，但說話者認為很重要，或者那件事和當下話題十分相關的事。句型 2 當作感嘆詞的「欸」有上揚語調和下降語調的用法。上揚語調的「欸」表示說話者覺得疑惑或是出乎意料之外。下降語調的「欸」用在親近的朋友和兄弟姊妹之間，表示說話者想喚起別人的注意，希望對方注意自己的存在或是要聽話者注意接下來要說的話。如果說話的對象是不熟識的人或是年紀比自己大的人，會讓人感覺不禮貌。

　　"eh" is used at the end of a statement to imply that the speaker is going to say something that the listener does not know, but the speaker thinks is important or relevant to the on-going matter. "eh" is also used as an interjection. When it is said with a rising intonation, it indicates that the speaker is confused or surprised. "eh" with a falling intonation is used between close friends and within siblings. It indicates that the speaker is trying to get someone's attention, either to notice his/her presence or to ask the listener to pay attention to what he/she is about to say. If the interlocutor is a stranger or a person older than the speaker, it gives an impression of impoliteness.

1 | 句型 1

1.1 | A：你很奇怪欸，為什麼這麼冷還要開窗戶？

B：就很熱咩。

1.2 | A：這杯果汁沒加糖嗎？很酸欸！

B：不夠甜的話，糖在這裡，你自己加。

2 | 句型 2

2.1 | **上揚語調**

A：欸？這裡以前不是一家大飯店嗎？

B：那家飯店五年前倒了，現在是電影院了。

2.2 | **下降語調**

A：欸，你幫我把衛生紙拿過來好嗎？

B：廁所裡面的都用完啦？

1 | Pattern 1

1.1 | A：You are weird. Why do you open the window when it's so cold?

B：It's just hot for me.

1.2 | A：Is this juice unsweetened? It's so sour.

B：If it's not sweet enough, here's the sugar, help yourself.

2 | Pattern 2

2.1 | **Rising intonation**

A：Hey? Wasn't there a big hotel here before?

B：That hotel went bankrupt five years ago. It's a movie theater now.

2.2 | **Falling intonation**

A：Hey, can you help me get some toilet paper?

B：Are we out of toilet paper in the bathroom?

! 你知道嗎 Do you know

　　「欸」在中國字典裡標註的是「āi」，但在台灣的字典標註的是「èi」的音，「唉」才是「āi」是嘆氣的擬聲語氣詞。「欸」在台灣華語中的使用頻率頗高，可能是受到台語的影響，而它在台語中就是發「eh」的音，也是說話者出乎意料之外時用的語氣詞。巧合的是，在日語中，感到出乎意外的時候也會發出「へ～～ (e)」的上揚語調聲音。

　　In a Chinese dictionary, " 欸 " is transcribed as "āi", but it is transcribed as "èi" in a Taiwanese dictionary, and "唉" is transcribed as "āi", which is onomatopoeia for "sigh". In Táiwān Huáyǔ, "eh" is used quite frequently, and probably because of the influence of the Taiwanese language. In Taiwanese, it is also used when a speaker is surprised. Coincidentally, Japanese speakers also make a rising intonation of " へ～～ (e)" when they are surprised.

NOTE

I. 選擇：根據對話，選擇一個最適當的語氣詞。

Multiple choice: According to the dialogue, choose the most appropriate modal particle.

（　　）1｜A：你天天被老闆罵，不換工作嗎？

　　　　　　　B：換一個會更好嗎？_____，我也不知道。

　　　　　　　(a) 咧　(b) 唉　(c) 啦　(d) 咩

（　　）2｜A：這裡離公園很近，很安靜，還有一個小學在附近。

　　　　　　　　車站_____，也是走路十分鐘就到了。

　　　　　　　B：聽起來不錯。

　　　　　　　(a) 唉　(b) 咩　(c) 欸　(d) 咧

（　　）3｜A：你怎麼每天都吃樓下賣的涼麵，不膩嗎？

　　　　　　　B：就方便_____。不然你幫我去買別的。

　　　　　　　(a) 咩　(b) 咧　(c) 啦　(d) 捏

（　　）4｜A：我等一下還有事，要先走了。

　　　　　　　B：這是你最喜歡的巧克力蛋糕_____。你不吃一塊再走嗎？

　　　　　　　(a) 唉　(b) 咩　(c) 捏　(d) 嘛

（　　）5｜A：_____，你的筆掉了。

　　　　　　　B：謝謝你。

　　　　　　　(a) 咩　(b) 嘛　(c) 欸　(d) 唉

II. 選出適合的交談對話內容：

Choose the appropriate conversation content:

（　　）1｜A：他為什麼大學畢業了還跟父母住在一起？

　　　　　　　B：❶ 一個人住很好捏。

　　　　　　　　❷ 他就不想花錢租房子咩。

（　）2｜A：你知道小李現在在做什麼嗎？好久沒有他的消息了。

B：❶ 欸，他的手機幾號啊？

❷ 我也不知道。我換工作以後就跟他沒聯絡了咧。

（　）3｜A：❶ 欸？火車不是四點半的嗎？

❷ 好吃的東西就要慢慢吃咩。

B：不是，是四點的，快來不及了！

（　）4｜A：來來來，兩件五百，高貴不貴，要買要快。

B：❶ 唉，今天賣得不太好嘛。

❷ 老闆，前面有一攤賣三件五百捏。

▶ 挑戰你自己：用語氣詞「咧／咩／欸」延伸上面任何一個對話。

Challenge yourself: Use modal particle lie / mie / ài to extend any of the dialogues above.

:: **情境例句 Contextual Example**　　　🎧 MP3-040

A：你下個星期會去參加籃球比賽
　　齁。
B：你到時候要來幫我加油喔。

A：You're going to the basketball game next week, huh.
B：You'll have to come cheer me on then.

:: **句型 Sentence Pattern**

1｜S＋齁
2｜……A 齁、B 齁、C 齁，……
3｜……NP／VP＋齁，……
4｜吼（感嘆詞）

:: **用法 Usage**

　　句型 1、句型 2 和句型 3 的「齁」有說話者邀請聽話者商量或確認的意味，使得無論是要求、命令、建議、鼓勵、拒絕，在態度上都顯得比較客氣和緩。雖然「齁」的功能是說話者邀請聽話者商量或確認，但除非是訊息有錯誤，聽話者一般不需要回應。當說話者要說一段比較長的言論時，「齁」往往大量出現，讓整段話聽起來像是兩個人的交談互動，除了能確認聽話者是不是正確接收前面所說的話，同時也藉此幫助說話者自己講出更深入的內容。句型 4 當作感嘆詞的「吼」，也可以發成「hooh」的音，音量比一般語句大，表示說話人感到不耐煩或是說話人不喜歡某個情況的情緒反應。

　　"hohhn" in Pattern 1, Pattern 2 and Pattern 3 implies that the speaker is inviting the listener to discuss or confirm, which makes the attitude seem more courteous and gentler when requesting, commanding, suggesting, encouraging, or refusing. Although the speaker invites the listener to discuss or confirm by using "hohhn", the listener usually does not respond to the request unless the message is wrong. When the speaker makes a long talk, "hohhn" tends to appear a lot, which makes the speech sound like a conversation between two people. This helps to check whether the listener has received correctly what the speaker has said and helps the speaker go deeper into the content. In Pattern 4, "hohhn" is used as an interjection, and can be pronounced as "hooh". It is pronounced louder than usual talking. It expresses a feeling of impatience or unpleasantness for the speaker.

:: 例句 Example

1 | 句型 1

1.1 | A：你在工廠工作很辛苦齁？

B：有什麼工作不辛苦的嗎？

1.2 | A：咖啡喝完了，你現在去買好不好？

B：等一下，我先把這個報告寫完齁。

2 | 句型 2

2.1 | 台灣有很多米做的小吃，米糕齁、碗粿齁、蘿蔔糕齁，夜市都有賣。

2.2 | 那個公寓什麼家具都有了，床齁、沙發齁、桌子齁，都又新又好。你只要帶行李過去就可以了。

1 | Pattern 1

1.1 | A：It's hard work at the factory, huh?

B：Is there any work that is not hard?

1.2 | A：I'm out of coffee. Can you go buy some now?

B：Wait a moment, let me finish this report first.

2 | Pattern 2

2.1 | There are many snacks made from rice in Taiwan, such as rice cake, savory rice pudding, and turnip cake, they are sold at night market.

2.2 | The apartment has all the furniture: bed, sofa, and table – they are all new and nice. You just need to bring your luggage. It will be fine.

第二單元：語氣助詞

PART II: Modal Particles

3 | 句型 3

3.1 | 網路購物很方便是很方便，可是我覺得齁，如果是衣服或是鞋子，不能試穿，也不能摸到東西，實在沒有把握。雖然說可以退齁，但是還是有點麻煩。我還是比較喜歡去店裡面買。

3.2 | 健康保險真的很重要，要是沒有齁，沒有錢的人生了病就不敢去看醫生，因為會擔心花很多錢。可是這樣有的時候不只對生病的那個人不好，也可能對別人不安全。

4 | 句型 4

4.1 | A：吼，怎麼這樣開車，到底會不會開啊？

B：就是咩，要右轉也不打方向燈。

4.2 | A：星期五考第三課到第六課。

B：吼，老師，太多了啦。

3 | Pattern 3

3.1 | It's very convenient to shop online, but I think I'm not sure about buying clothes or shoes online. You can't try them on or touch them. Although it is ok to return the goods, it is still a bit troublesome. I still prefer to buy from the store.

3.2 | Health insurance is really important. If there is no health insurance, people with no money will not dare to see a doctor when they are sick because they will worry about spending a lot of money. But sometimes this is not only bad for the sick person, but it may also be unsafe for others.

4 | Pattern 4

4.1 | A： Sheesh, how can he drive like this? Does he know how to drive?

B： Yeah, he doesn't use the turning signal to turn right.

4.2 | A： The test on Friday will cover chapter 3 to 6.

B： Oh, sir, it's too much.

課本沒教的台灣華語句型50

！原來如此 No Wonder

　　人類說話不只是單一方向的給出訊息，而是一個和聽話者一起合作參與的複雜動態過程，所以談話的雙方必須在說什麼、怎麼說、對方知道的背景知識等各個層面找到共識、協商合作，以便隨時調整說話的方向，來保持交談的順利。因此在這個過程中自然可能引發具有邀請對方參與說話、共同協商功能的句尾或詞尾「齁」大量出現。特別是命令、警告或是語氣緩和的建議、鼓勵之類的祈使句，是對聽話者的行動自由的干預，有了「齁」的使用，意味著自己的陳述是和聽話者一起協商出來的結果。簡單來說，言談中使用「齁」就是一種禮貌策略的運用。

　　Human speech is not just a one-way message. Rather it is a complex and dynamic process in which both the speaker and the listener cooperate and participate. Therefore, both parties must find a consensus on what to say, how to say it, and what each other knows – background knowledge – so that they can adjust the direction of the conversation at any time and keep it going smoothly. Therefore, it is natural that "hohhn" in the end of sentences or words appears a lot during the process of conversation to encourage the other party into participating and negotiating. In particular, imperative sentences for orders, warnings, soft suggestions, or encouragement are interventions to the freedom of action of the listener, and the use of "hohhn" signifies that the statement in fact results from negotiation with the listener. In other words, using "hohhn" in speech is a politeness strategy.

19　蛤 hahhn

:: 情境例句 Contextual Example　　　　∩ MP3-042

A：表演結束以後，我請你去吃飯
　　蛤。
B：太好了，我們去吃牛排。

A：A: After the show ends, I'll treat you
　　to dinner.
B：Great. Let's go get steaks.

:: 句型 Sentence Pattern

1｜S＋蛤
2｜蛤？（感嘆詞）

:: 用法 Usage

　　句型 1 的語氣詞「蛤」有高音，也有低音，都是說話者希望得到聽話者正面的肯定，或是可以執行或遵守他的要求，高音比低音顯得更熱切一點，可以用在陳述句，也可以用在疑問句。句型 2 的感嘆詞「蛤」，單獨使用在以下三種情況：一是沒聽清楚對方說的話；二是對對方說的話感到疑惑；三是感到驚訝的時候。

　　In Pattern 1, "hahhn" can be high- or low-pitched. In both cases, it signifies that the speaker wants to receive positive affirmation from the listener or to be able to carry out or comply with his or her demands. The high-pitched "hahhn" sounds more enthusiastic than the low one. In Pattern 2, "hahhn" is used by itself as an interjection when: 1) the speaker does not hear clearly what the interlocutor is saying; 2) the speaker is confused by what the interlocutor is saying; or 3) the speaker is surprised at what the interlocutor is saying.

1 | 句型 1

1.1 | A： （送客時）有空再來玩蛤。

B：好，一定一定。

1.2 | A： 今天會不會下雨蛤？要帶
傘嗎？

B：很難說，還是帶著吧。

2 | 句型 2

2.1 | A： 這些錢是要付下個學期的
學費的。

B：蛤？

2.2 | A： 蛤？明天要下雪？

B：是啊，這裡很少下雪的。

2.3 | A： 經理說今年六月開始一個
星期上班四天！

B：蛤？怎麼可能？星期五要
在家上班吧？

1 | Pattern 1

1.1 | A： *(Seeing guests off)* Come to play
again when you have time.

B： Okay, I will.

1.2 | A： Is it going to rain today? Do I
need to bring an umbrella?

B： It's hard to say. You'd better
bring it.

2 | Pattern 2

2.1 | A： A: This money is for the tuition
of the next semester.

B： What?

2.2 | A： Huh? Is it going to snow
tomorrow?

B： Yes, it rarely snows here.

2.3 | A： The manager said that we will
work four days a week starting
from June this year!

B： Huh? How can it be? We have
to work from home on Friday,
right?

　　用在陳述句末和疑問句末的「蛤」可以用「啊」來替換，不過「啊」意味說話者投入很多自己的主觀和感情，用這樣來促使（但沒有一定要）聽話者做出回應，和「蛤」要求聽話者給出肯定認同的回應有一點不同。比方說，A：「哇！這個房間怎麼這麼髒啊？」跟 B：「哇！這個房間怎麼這麼髒蛤？」聽話者可以不回應 A，可是卻要回應 B。因此，反問句不需要聽話者回應，跟「蛤」的用法矛盾，所以「蛤」不用在反問句尾。聽不清楚或對對方說的話疑惑、驚訝或是懷疑時，普通話用的是「什麼？」。

"hahhn" can be replaced with "a" at the end of a statement or a question. However, "a" implies that the speaker puts a lot of subjectivity and emotion of his or her own, which prompts (but does not necessarily require) a response from the listener, whereas "hahhn" requests an affirmative recognition from the listener. That is the difference between "a" and "hahhn." For example, A: "Wa! zhè ge fángjiān zěnme zhème zāng a? (Wow! Why is this room so dirty)?" whereas B: "Wa! zhè ge fángjiān zěnme zhème zāng hahhn?" The listener can have no response to A but will respond to B. Therefore, the rhetorical question does not require a response from the listener, which is contradictory to the use of "hahhn", so "hahhn" does not appear at the end of the rhetorical question. When a speaker does not hear clearly what the interlocutor is saying or is confused, surprised, or suspicious of what the interlocutor is saying, the speaker says "shénme 'what'" in Pǔtōnghuà.

NOTE

20　hioh

:: **情境例句** Contextual Example　　　　🎧 MP3-044

A：你已經照了五分鐘了，還照
　　啊？你是沒照過相 hioh？

B：這裡太美了嘛，第一次來，當
　　然要多照幾張。

A：You've been taking pictures for 5
　　minutes. You are taking more? Have
　　you never taken pictures before?

B：It's so beautiful here, and this is the
　　first time I came here. Sure I have to
　　take more pictures.

:: **句型** Sentence Pattern

1 | S ＋ hioh？
2 | hioh（感嘆詞）

:: **用法** Usage

　　「hioh」是要求聽話者確認的疑問語氣詞，也用在不需要聽話者回應的反問
句。反問句的「hioh」是用來引起聽話者的注意，凸顯說話者的立場來達到反
駁、指責的目的，句子裡的主語後可以加上「是」來加強語氣。句型 2 感嘆詞
「hioh」可以單獨使用，表示說話者聽到了對方所說的。但是如果「hioh」之後
沒有再說別的跟對方所說有關的事情，容易讓人感覺說話者的態度敷衍、冷淡。
因為「hioh」這個語音不是華語可能的發音組合，所以沒有漢字可以代表，有的
時候影音作品的字幕上會看到以台灣人常用的注音符號「ㄏㄧㄡ」來表示。

　　"hioh" is an interrogative particle for a question that requests the listener to
confirm what the speaker said. It is also used in rhetorical questions that do not need
the listener to respond. In a rhetorical question, "hioh" is used to draw the listener's
attention so the speaker's point of view is noticed, and his purpose of rebuttal and
accusation can be achieved. It can collocate with "shì", which is placed after a subject,
to emphasize the tone. In Pattern 2, when "hioh" is used alone as an interjection, it
signifies the speaker's acknowledging of what the interlocutor has said. However, if
nothing else is said after "hioh", it gives the impression that the speaker is perfunctory
and indifferent. Because the pronunciation "hioh" is not a possible phonetic

課本沒教的台灣華語句型50

combination in Mandarin, there is no character to represent it. Sometimes it is typed as " ㄏ 一 ㄡ " in video captions in Bopomofo, the Mandarin phonetic transcription system used in Taiwan.

:: **例句 Example**   🎧 MP3-045

1 | 句型 1

1.1 | **問句**

A：臉這麼臭，你被老闆罵了 hioh？

B：唉，別提了，老闆叫我要重做昨天的企劃案。

1.2 | **反問句**

A：幫我把外套拿過來。

B：今天又不冷，穿這麼多，你是生病 hioh？

2 | 句型 2

2.1 | A：你看了這本雜誌說台灣是地球上最危險的地方嗎？

B：hioh，還沒看，我只感覺好吃的東西太多，對我的體重很危險。

2.2 | A：我明天要去爬玉山，好期待喔。

B：hioh。

1 | Pattern 1

1.1 | **Question**

A： Why the long face? Were you scolded by the boss?

B： Sigh, don't mention it. My boss asked me to redo yesterday's proposal.

1.2 | **Rhetorical question**

A： Please bring me my coat over.

B： It's not cold today. You wear so much. Are you sick?

2 | Pattern 2

2.1 | A： Have you read this magazine, which said that Taiwan is the most dangerous place on earth?

B： Oh, I haven't read it yet. I just feel that there are too many tasty things, which are dangerous to my weight.

2.2 | A： I'm going to climb Jade Mountain tomorrow. I'm so looking forward to it.

B： I see.

! 原來如此 No Wonder

「齁」、「蛤」、「hioh」這三個語氣詞都是從台語而來的，一般的華語字典查不到這三個字實際上的口語發音，這裡所標注的發音是常用的「台語羅馬拼音」。「齁」和「蛤」這兩個字是現在常見代表這兩個音的漢字，並不是正規的台語漢字。「Hohhn」除了「齁」也常見寫成「吼」，特別是當感嘆詞的時候。「齁」和「蛤」在普通話中沒有相應的語氣詞，而「hioh」相當於普通話在句末附加「是嗎？」來要求對方確認「hioh」之前所說的內容。

The pronunciation of these three particles "hohhn," "hahhn," and "hioh" are all from the language Taiwanese. They cannot be found in general Mandarin dictionaries. The two characters " 齁 " and " 蛤 " are now commonly-used Chinese characters that represent these two sounds. They are not standard Taiwanese characters. "hohhn" is also commonly written as " 吼 ," especially when it is used as an interjection. In Pǔtōnghuà, " 齁 " and " 蛤 " have no equivalent words. "hioh" is equivalent to adding "shì ma?" at the end of a sentence in Pǔtōnghuà in order to ask the interlocutor to acknowledge the sentence before "hioh."

NOTE

I. 填空：根據對話，選擇一個最適當的語氣詞。

Fill in the blanks: According to the dialogue, choose the most appropriate modal particle.

a 齁　|　b 蛤　|　c hioh

1｜A：我想吃你做的菜已經想了好久了，好好吃喔。

　　B：好吃＿＿＿＿。多吃點。

2｜A：我昨天去看馬友友的音樂會耶！他的表演真棒！

　　B：＿＿＿＿。晚上要吃什麼？

3｜A：點心在桌上＿＿＿＿。我出門了。

　　B：喔。再見。

4｜A：點珍珠奶茶的時候，你可以說你要的甜度，看是要全糖、半糖、
　　　微糖還是無糖＿＿＿＿，也可以選要多少冰塊，正常冰還是少冰還
　　　是去冰。

　　B：這樣啊，那我就不擔心每天喝一杯了。

5｜A：耶！進球了！5：4了！

　　B：你是幫哪一邊加油的＿＿＿＿？

II. 選出適合的交談對話內容：

Choose the appropriate conversation content:

（　　）1｜A：說！你為什麼十點半才回來？

　　　　　B：我在學校圖書館寫報告啊。

　　　　　A：❶ 圖書館幾點關蛤？

　　　　　　　❷ 你是當我是小孩子 hioh？學校圖書館九點就關了。

（　）2｜A：❶ 等一下我們要看的博物館裡面比較冷，要是你怕冷、容易感冒的人，帶一件外套齁。

❷ 明天早上七點吃早餐，八點出發蛤。

B：導遊先生我們幾點回到車上？

A：我們在這裡停一個小時，四點半上車。

（　）3｜A：❶ 她很漂亮齁。很多人都喜歡她。

❷ 姐，你不要這樣看我啦！我喜歡她很明顯 hioh？

B：哈哈哈，你喜歡她大概連瞎子都看得出來吧。

（　）4｜A：公司下個月十五號要辦聖誕派對。你打算穿什麼？

B：❶ 蛤？什麼時候？

❷ 準備好再來齁。

▶ 挑戰你自己：用語氣詞「齁／蛤／hioh」延伸上面任何一個對話。

Challenge yourself: Use modal particle hohhn / hahhn / hioh to extend any of the dialogues above.

流行語句型

　　流行語是新生的語言內容，是隨著流行事物的出現自然發生的，也是文化的一部分。它記錄並且反映了一個地方某個時期的社會狀況或是價值觀念，來源有廣告、電影電視、新聞事件、網路社交媒體等等。使用的時間可能很短，也可能演化成新的詞彙存留下來成為常態。有的只流行在特定的年齡族群，有的會擴散到其他年齡層，有的甚至成為大眾仿效的句型。這裡收集了十個近二十年來在台灣常見的流行語，以及從這些流行語中提取出來的句型，其中，第 21–23 個句型是從影視作品來的，第 24–27 個句型是從網路論壇來的，第 28–30 個句型是從新聞事件來的，這個單元將介紹這些流行語的出處，以及從這些流行語產生的句型和它們的用法。

Catch Phrase Patterns

Catch phrases are new language content. They naturally emerge with popular and trendy things and are a part of culture as well. They record and reflect the history of a society or the values of a period of time in a place. Sources of catch phrases are various, including advertisements, movies and TV programs, news events, social media, etc. The lifespan of a catch phrase may be very short, or it may last longer and evolve into a new word and survive to become the norm. Some are only popular within certain age groups; some will spread to more age groups, and some become sentence patterns imitated by the public. Here is a collection of ten catch phrases that have been popular in Taiwan in the last two decades, as well as sentence patterns extracted from these catch phrases. Pattern 21–23 come from film and television, Pattern 24–27 come from online forums, and Pattern 28–30 come from news events. This part will introduce the sources of these catch phrases, the sentence patterns generated from these phrases, and their usages.

21 你的 X 不是你的 X your X is not your X

:: **原文例句 Original Sentence**　　　🎧 MP3-047

你的孩子不是你的孩子。

Your child is not yours.

:: **出處 Source**

　　《你的孩子不是你的孩子》是 2018 播出改編自同名小說的台灣電視劇。這齣電視劇是由五個帶有科幻元素的故事組合起來的，劇情主要是探討母親與孩子的關係，以及對教育、成就的迷思。劇裡的五位母親對成功的定義有著僵固的想法，要孩子學習好、考試成績好、上好學校，所以用有形或者無形的高壓方式控制、教育孩子，造成親子關係緊張，甚至導致孩子人格扭曲或者失去生命。「你的孩子不是你的孩子」的意思是你生養的孩子並不是你所擁有的東西，孩子有他自己的生命，是個獨立的個體。

> ### 重點詞彙 Keywords
>
> · **控制 kòngzhì**　　*v.*　　to control
> · **教育 jiàoyù**　　*n. / v.*　　education; to educate

On Children (2018, lit. *Your Child is not Your Child*) is a Taiwanese TV series adapted from a novel of the same name. This TV series is composed of five stories with science fiction elements. The plot mainly explores the relationship between mothers and children, as well as myths about education and success. The five mothers in the series have rigid thought about the definition of success. They want their children to study hard, get good grades, and go to good schools. Therefore, they use tangible or intangible high-pressure ways to control and to educate their children. This causes tension in each parent-child relationship, leading to their children's personalities being distorted or their lives lost. "Your child is not your child" means that the child you gave birth to and nurtured is not your possession. A child has his / her own life and is an independent individual.

111

你的＋N＋不是你的＋N

　　描述某個屬於你的人、事或物不是表面看到的那樣,還有另一個層次的意義。

This pattern is used to describe a person or a thing that belongs to you is not what you see on the surface but has another level of meaning.

:: 例句 Example　　　　　　　　　　　∩ MP3-048

1 | 房子太貴了,你的房子不是你的房子,就算你買了房子,還有一大筆的房貸。	1 | A house is too expensive. Your house is not yours. Even if you buy a house, you still have a large mortgage.
2 | 你的工作不是你的工作嗎?你該想想換一個你真的喜歡的工作了。	2 | Feeling like your job is not yours? You should think about changing to a job you truly like.
3 | 你的父母不是你的父母,他們還有很多其他的身分,不可能總是照顧著你。	3 | Your parents are not your parents. They have many other roles and cannot always take care of you.

第三單元：流行語句型

PART III: Catch Phrase Patterns

A 與 B 的距離 The distance between A and B

:: **原文例句 Original Sentence**　　　🎧 MP3-049

我們與惡的距離到底有多遠？　　　How far are we from evil?

:: **出處 Source**

　　《我們與惡的距離》是台灣 2019 年播出的社會寫實電視劇。劇情描述一個隨機殺人的事件發生以後，不同角色的心境與遭遇。一位人權律師想找出兇手的行凶動機，但是不被大眾與親人理解。加害人的家屬為了躲避社會的指摘和自我的譴責，艱難地生活著。被害人之一的母親走不出傷痛，與家人的關係緊張。還有一位精神疾病患者，也可能是潛在的犯罪者。每一集都是以一則電視新聞報導開始，接著浮現出網路上對該新聞的批評謾罵，就像現實社會一樣，使觀眾在看劇同時也思考是否我們與惡的距離並非想像中的那麼遠。

重點詞彙 Keywords

· 惡　　è　　*n.*　evil
· 距離　jùlí　*n.*　distance

The World Between Us (2019, lit. *The Distance Between Us and Evil*) is a Taiwanese TV drama. The plot is about the feelings and encounters of different characters after a random mass killing. A human rights lawyer wanted to find out the murderer's motive, but he was not understood by the public and his families. The family of the perpetrator lived a difficult life because of social criticism and self-condemnation. A mother of one of the victims was unable to get out of the pain, and caused tension with other family members. Another character had a mental health problem and could be a potential offender. Each episode starts with a TV news report, and then criticism about the news on the Internet floats on the screen, which is just like real society. This makes the audience think that the distance between us and evil may not be as far as we imagine.

:: 句型 Sentence Pattern

N ＋ 與 ＋ N ＋ 的距離

:: 用法 Usage

　　描述兩個事物的遠近，或者要討論兩個事物之間的關係或差別，後者多用在文章的標題。

This is used to describe the distance between two things, or to discuss the relationship or difference between two things. The latter is mostly used in the title of an article.

:: 例句 Example

🎧 MP3-050

1 | 有很多錢可以拉近我們與快樂的距離嗎？

1 | Can money bring us closer to happiness if we own a lot of it?

2 | 學習與考試的距離不只是成績而已。

2 | The distance between learning and exam is not just grades.

3 | 台灣每一次的總統選舉都在決定「台灣與中國的距離」。

3 | Every presidential election in Taiwan determines the "distance between Taiwan and China."

:: 原文例句 Original Sentence　　　　🎧 MP3-051

你是忘記了，還是害怕想起來？

Have you forgotten? Or are you too afraid to remember?

:: 出處 Source

　　原文是出自 2019 年電影《返校》。這是從一個同名的電腦遊戲改編的台灣校園懸疑歷史驚悚片。故事敘述在 1962 年，當時台灣還是戒嚴時代，政府以維護國家安全之名，對人民實行高壓統治，管控所有人的思想，限制人民自由。一所高中裡有一群學生和兩位老師組成讀書會閱讀禁書，後來遭到校園教官揪舉而受到逮捕，讀書會裡幾乎所有人都被凌虐致死，使得校園裡有很多受冤害的鬼魂，最後僅有一人存活下來作為這段殘暴歷史的見證。

重點詞彙 Keywords

· 戒嚴 **jièyán**　*v.*　to enforce martial law
· 逮補 **dàibǔ**　*v.*　to arrest

　　The sentence is from the movie *Detention* (2019), a historical suspense thriller adapted from a computer game of the same name. The story takes place in a Taiwanese high school in 1962, when Taiwan was still under martial law. The government, in the name of national security, ruled oppressively over its people, controlling everyone's thought and restricting their freedom. In the high school, a group of students and two teachers formed a book club to read banned books. They were caught by a school military instructor, and later almost all of them were arrested and tortured to death by the secret police. Therefore, the campus is full of ghosts of victims; however, one student survived as a witness to that cruel history.

:: 句型 Sentence Pattern

你是＋ V（＋了）＋還是＋ VP ？

:: 用法 Usage

　　以反問句的形式來質問別人，一般來說，「還是」以後的語句才是說話者真正想要表達的意思。

　　This pattern is used in a rhetorical question to challenge someone. The main idea that a speaker intends to convey usually is the phrase after "háishì (or)."

:: 例句 Example

1 | 什麼！？你的罰單還沒繳？你是忘了，還是故意不繳？

1 | What!? You haven't paid your ticket? Did you forget, or did you deliberately not pay?

2 | 你的行李箱壞了那麼久還沒修，你是沒錢修，還是擔心修不好？

2 | Your suitcase has been broken for so long and still hasn't been fixed. Do you have no money to fix it, or are you worried that it won't be fixed?

3 | 你不是很喜歡阿美嗎？今天怎麼沒跟她說話？你是沒看到她，還是太害羞？

3 | Don't you like A Mei very much? Why didn't you talk to her today? Did you not see her, or were you too shy?

第三單元：流行語句型

PART III: Catch Phrase Patterns

I. 流行話填空

Fill in the blanks:

> a 與惡的距離 | b 不是你的貓 | c 藝術 |
>
> d 你的孩子 | e 還是害怕想起來

1 | 你的貓 ＿＿＿＿，而是你需要服務、照顧的家人。

2 | 你小的時候一練鋼琴就大哭，你是忘記了，＿＿＿＿？

3 | ＿＿＿＿不是你的孩子，孩子有自己的興趣，父母不能總是要孩子聽他們的話。

4 | 我們 ＿＿＿＿可能沒有你想的那麼遠，如果我們在網上不注意自己說的話，也有可能讓別人受傷。

5 | ＿＿＿＿與不是藝術的距離是你看得懂看不懂，但是我不知道看得懂的是藝術，還是看不懂的才是藝術呢？

II. 對話配對
Conversation pairing:

1｜現在手機越來越進步，你
的手機不是你的手機，它
還可以是你車子的鑰匙。

2｜這次的考試怎麼考得那麼
差？是老師教的你聽不
懂，還是你沒認真念書？

3｜聰明的老師可以拉近遊戲
與學習的距離。

4｜開會沒有準備午餐！？你
是沒有被通知到，還是第
一天工作？

5｜現在做什麼事都有網路幫
忙，真方便！

A｜對不起，我馬上去準備。

B｜不過，你的生活不是你的
生活，網路影響你比你想
的更多。

C｜真的嗎？可是我的車子還
沒有那麼進步，我的手機
還不能開車門。

D｜我會更努力的，下次一定
考好。

E｜如果老師們都能懂就好
了。

▶ 挑戰你自己：用「你的 X 不是你的 X ／ A 與 B 的距離／你是 A，
還是 B ？」完成下面的任務。
Challenge yourself: complete the task below with one of these patterns: nǐ
de X bú shì nǐ de X / A yǔ B de jùlí / nǐ shì A, háishì B?

你和朋友約十點見面，他十點半還沒來。你打電話跟他說什
麼？

24　把 X 當塑膠　Look down upon X

:: **原文例句 Original Sentence**　　🎧 MP3-054

不要把年輕人當塑膠。

Don't treat young people as plastic.
(Don't look down upon young people.)

:: **出處 Source**

　　原文是 2020 年台灣青少年發明的流行語，「被當塑膠」的意思是被忽略、被輕視或無視，也有被當作不存在的意思。在 1980 年代台灣經濟快速發展的時期，高雄生產了很多石化產品，塑膠是其中之一。塑化材料很容易複製而且價格低廉，因此取代了很多石頭、木材、金屬等製作商品的天然材料，但是做出來的產品往往讓人有粗糙、廉價的印象。因此「被當塑膠」或「是塑膠做的」，就是指某人事物像是被當作塑膠做的廉價品一樣，有被貶低、覺得不好、沒有用的意涵。另外，因為塑膠可以是透明的，所以也帶有被忽視、輕視的含意。現在這個流行語也擴散到青少年以外的年齡層，而且經常出現在媒體上。

重點詞彙 Keywords

· **塑膠 sùjiāo**　*n.*　plastic
· **無視 wúshì**　*v.*　to ignore

The original sentence is a catch phrase invented by teenagers in Taiwan in 2020. "To be treated as plastic" means to be ignored, belittled, or to be regarded as invisible. During the 1980s, Taiwan's economy was developing rapidly. Many petrochemical products were produced in Kaohsiung, and plastic was one of them. Plastic is easy and inexpensive to replicate, so it replaces many natural materials such as stone, wood, and metal, but it gives the impression that the products are poorly-made and cheap. Thus, "bèi dāng sùjiāo (being treated as plastic)" or "shì sùjiāo zuò de (made of plastic)" is like being treated as a cheap product made of plastic. In addition, plastic can be transparent. Hence it gained the connotation of being ignored or belittled. Now the usage of this catch phrase has also spread to age groups other than teenagers, and it appears in the media a lot.

:: 句型 Sentence Pattern

把＋ N ＋當塑膠 或
N ＋當＋ N ＋（是）＋塑膠 或
N ＋不是塑膠做的

:: 用法 Usage

經常以反問句或否定的形式，用在生氣或吵架的時候。說話者內心真正的想法是：不要以為我好欺負。

This pattern is often used in rhetorical questions or negative sentences during angry exchanges or quarreling. What the speaker has in mind is this: don't think I am easy to bully.

:: 例句 Example

🎧 MP3-055

1 ｜ 結婚這麼重要的事你幫我決定，你當我塑膠嗎？

1 ｜ Marriage is such an important matter, and you decide for me. Do you belittle me?

2 ｜ 為什麼這個三明治裡面的蛋只有這麼一小塊？你們當顧客是塑膠喔？

2 ｜ Why is only such a small piece of egg in this sandwich? Do you think customers don't care?

3 ｜ 這個危險的東西是誰放在這裡的？好像把大樓管理辦法當塑膠一樣。

3 ｜ Who put this dangerous thing here? It's like ignoring the building's management measures.

4 ｜台灣不是塑膠做的！台灣人會自己保護自己的。

4 ｜ Taiwan is no pushover! Taiwanese will defend ourselves.

25 | X 躺著也中槍 X is caught in a crossfire

:: **原文例句 Original Sentence** 🎧 MP3-056

哇靠，躺著都能中槍。 Damn, I got caught in the crossfire.

:: **出處 Source**

　　原文是出自 2012 年香港喜劇電影《逃學威龍》裡的一句台詞。電影劇情裡有一個片段是兩群人激烈打鬥，過程中有一個人躺著裝死，但是仍然被槍打中，所以說出了「躺著都中槍」這句話。現在經常說「躺著也中槍」來表示第三者無緣無故受到一件壞事的牽連，也可以縮略成「躺槍」。

重點詞彙 Keywords

· **中槍 zhòngqiāng** *v.* to get shot
· **牽連 qiānlián** *v.* to be involved

　　The sentence is from a line in the Hong Kong comedy movie *Fighting Back to School* (2012). In the movie, there is a scene of two groups of people fighting fiercely. During the fighting, a person lay down and pretended to be dead, but he still got shot. Hence, he said the phrase "tǎng zhe dōu zhòng qiāng 'getting shot while laying down'." Nowadays, it is often said "tǎng zhe yě zhòng qiāng" to indicate that a third party has been implicated in a bad thing for no reason. It can also be shortened as "tǎngqiāng."

:: **句型 Sentence Pattern**

N ＋躺著也／都中槍

:: **用法 Usage**

　　用來描述某人被無緣無故受到牽連，也可以用在自我解嘲，表示自己的無辜。

It is used to describe someone being implicated for no reason. It can also be used to ridicule oneself to express one's innocence.

:: **例句 Example**　　　　　　　　　　　　　🎧 MP3-057

1 | 小林的工作沒做完，經理要阿明留下來幫他，阿明真是躺著也中槍。

1 | Xiao Lin's work is not done. The manager asks A Ming to stay and help him. A Ming is really caught in the crossfire.

2 | 妹妹今天躺著也中槍，因為哥哥比賽輸了，心情不好，對她說話很不客氣。

2 | My elder brother took it out on younger sister. He lost the game and was in a bad mood, so he spoke to her very impolitely.

3 | 阿美和男朋友吵架也怪我？！我躺著都中槍啊！

3 | I am to blame for the quarrel between A Mei and her boyfriend?! I got caught in the crossfire.

先別管 A 了，你有聽過 B 嗎？
Don't mind A. Have you heard of B?

:: **原文例句 Original Sentence**　　　∩ MP3-058

先別管這個了，你有聽過安麗嗎？

Forget about this for now. Have you heard of Amway?

:: **出處 Source**

　　原文是 2012 年從台灣一個流量很大的網路電子佈告欄「PTT」開始流行的。因為很多人都有遇過直銷商安麗的推銷人員的經驗，對方往往先聊別的話題，然後才突然轉換主題，說：「你有聽過安麗嗎？」說了這句話以後，就開始促銷商品。後來引起許多人在「PTT」上模仿，用這個句型在一個句子裡說著不相干的兩件事，因為笑果十足而漸漸流行起來。這個句型前半部和後半部所說的話題通常是完全不相關的，有的時候只使用前半部，後半部換成「你知道……嗎？」或者是其他想要說的主題，而且不一定用疑問句。

> **重點詞彙 Keywords**
>
> · **話題 huàtí**　　*n.*　topic
> · **促銷 cùxiāo**　　*v.*　to promote (merchandise)

　　This sentence originated from PTT, a large-traffic Internet bulletin board in Taiwan, and has become very popular since 2012. This is the story: many people have the experience of meeting a salesperson from the multi-level marketing company Amway. The salesperson often talks about some random topic first and later suddenly changes the topic and says: "Have you heard of Amway?" After saying this, the salesperson starts promoting products. Later, many people began to mock this sentence pattern and wrote two points that were completely irrelevant in one sentence on PTT. It was hilarious, so this pattern gradually became popular. In this sentence pattern, the topics of the first half and the second half are usually completely unrelated. Sometimes only the first half of the pattern is used, and the second half is replaced with "nǐ zhīdào…

mā? (Do you know...)" or other topic that you want to talk about. It is not necessary to use interrogative sentences.

:: 句型 Sentence Pattern

先別管＋N／VP＋了，你＋有聽過／知道＋N／S＋嗎？　或
先別管＋N／VP＋了，S。

:: 用法 Usage

　　用來轉移聽話者的關注焦點。「先別管」後面接名詞，也可以用「這個」或「那個」來指正在談論的話題。社群媒體上也有用這個句型開頭的貼文，「先別管」後面的名詞一般是當時大家關注的事情。

　　This pattern is used to divert a listener's attention. The noun following "xiān bié guǎn (don't mind...)" can be the pronoun "zhè ge (this)" or "nà ge (that)" to refer to the on-going topic. There are posts on social media with this sentence pattern as an opening line. The nouns after "xiān bié guǎn" are generally what people concern about at that time.

:: 例句 Example　　　　　　　　　　　∩ MP3-059

1｜先別管語法了，你有聽過會說話的書嗎？

1｜Forget about grammar for now. Have you heard of books that speak (audible books)?

2｜先別管手機遊戲了，你知道小時候沒學過外國語長大也可以學得很好嗎？

2｜Don't mind mobile games for now. Do you know that you can still learn a foreign language very well even though you did not learn it when you were young?

3｜先別管吃什麼魚了，大學籃球比賽這個星期開始了。

3｜Forget about what fish we are going to eat for now. The college basketball game starts this week.

:: 原文例句 Original Sentence

🎧 MP3-060

我讀歷史我驕傲，我不會轉系的。

I major in history, and I am proud of it. I will not change my major.

:: 出處 Source

　　這個句型在中國非常普遍，意思是我因為某事、是某個地方的人或有某種認同等等而感到自豪，無論那是不是被社會主流所接受的價值。來源猜測跟一段表演台詞有關：2009 年中國春節聯歡晚會中一段叫作《吉祥三寶》的小品表演，當中有一個角色以從事保安（台灣說「保全」）工作為榮，說出：「身穿保安服，把門獻青春。我驕傲。」據此簡化成「我保安我驕傲」。隨著兩岸互動頻繁，這個句型也逐漸出現在台灣。2019 年 3 月屏東縣長和屏東鄉親們就在社群媒體上標註過「我屏東我驕傲」，這是因為當時屏東舉辦台灣燈會，約有 1300 萬參觀人次，創造了 131 億產值，活動非常成功。

重點詞彙 Keywords

· **驕傲 jiāo'ào** 　 v. 　 to be proud
· **標註 biāozhù** 　 v. 　 to tag

　　This sentence pattern is very common in China. It means that I am proud of something – the place I'm from, a certain identity, etc., whether it is a value accepted by the mainstream of society or not. It is speculated that the source is a line in the skit "Auspicious Three Treasures" in the 2009 Chinese New Year Gala in China. One of the characters was proud to work as a security guard and said "shēn chuān bǎo'ān fú, bǎ mén xiàn qīngchūn. wǒ jiāo'ào. (Wearing a security uniform and contributing my youth to watch doors. I am proud of it.)" Accordingly, it is simplified to "wǒ bǎo'ān wǒ jiāo'ào. (I am a guard, and I am proud of that.)" With the frequent interaction between the two sides of the Taiwan Strait, this sentence pattern has gradually spread in Taiwan. In

課本沒教的台灣華語句型50

March 2019, the Pingtung County Mayor and Pingtung villagers created the hashtag "wǒ Píngtōng wǒ jiāo'ào (I am from Pingtung, and I am proud of it.)" on social media. This is because the Taiwan Lantern Festival was held in Pingtung at that time. It attracted about 13 million visitors, and created NTD 1.31 billion output value to make the event very successful.

:: 句型 Sentence Pattern

我＋ N ／ VP ＋我驕傲

:: 用法 Usage

　　用來作為展現自我的態度，經常作為社群媒體的標籤或是活動標語。

　　This pattern is used to express an attitude of oneself. It is often used as social media hashtags or event slogans.

:: 例句 Example

🎧 MP3-061

1 | 我胖我驕傲，不用叫我減肥了。

1 | I'm fat, and I'm proud of it. No need to tell me to lose weight.

2 | 台南好吃的東西非常多，我台南我驕傲，歡迎到台南。

2 | There are so many tasty foods in Tainan. I am from Tainan, and I am proud of my hometown. Welcome to Tainan.

3 | 我會台語我驕傲，小的時候爺爺奶奶都跟我說台語，現在很多人都不會說了。

3 | I can speak Taiwanese, and I am proud of that. My grandparents spoke Taiwanese to me when I was young. Nowadays many people don't know how to speak Taiwanese.

I. 流行語填空
Fill in the blanks:

| a 當塑膠 | b 躺著也中槍 | c 我驕傲 | d 先別管 |

1 | 2020 年生活在台灣很安全，真的太幸福了！我住台灣_____！

2 | 我已經說了舞會晚上十點以前結束，現在都十一點半了還在吵，把我_____嗎？

3 | _____午餐吃什麼了，你知道那邊要開一家新的超市嗎？

4 | 妹妹功課沒做完，媽媽就不讓我們玩電腦遊戲，我和姐姐_____。

5 | 小明感覺到自己在班上被_____，沒什麼人要跟他玩、說話，可是老師、爸媽都還是很愛他。

II. 對話配對
Conversation pairing:

1 | 老王請阿明吃飯，可是叫我付錢。你說這樣對嗎？

2 | 我記者我驕傲，我寫了很多故事，讓需要幫忙的人被注意到。

3 | 洗衣機壞了，要換新的還是找人來看看？

4 | 誰把車停在這裡？把警察當塑膠嗎？

5 | 你會拿毛筆啊？現在已經很少人寫書法了。

A | 是啊，我學書法我驕傲。

B | 先別管洗衣機了，你有聽過地球暖化嗎？

C | 你真是躺着也中槍。

D | 就是嘛，停在這裡，大家怎麼進出呢？

E | 年輕人這樣很不錯，你的家人也會覺得驕傲的。

▶ 挑戰你自己：用「把 X 當塑膠／X 躺著也中槍／先別管 A 了」完成下面的任務。

Challenge yourself: complete the task below with one of these patterns: bǎ X dāng sùjiāo / X tǎngzhe yě zhòng qiāng / xiān bié guǎn A le

你的鄰居覺得昨天晚上是你帶朋友到家裡玩，把音樂開得很大聲，可是你並沒有，你怎麼告訴朋友這件事？

28　政治歸政治，X 歸 X
Politics belong to politics, X belongs to X

:: **原文例句 Original Sentence**　　　🎧 MP3-063

政治的歸政治，體育的歸體育。

Politics belong to politics, and sports belong to sports.

:: **出處 Source**

　　原文出現在 1994 年台灣總統府發言人的一句評論。當年亞洲奧運會已經發函邀請當時的總統李登輝出席在日本廣島舉行的第十二屆亞洲運動會，可是受到中國政府阻擾。中國國家主席江澤民恐嚇說如果李總統出席，中國隊就退賽。後來當時科威特籍的奧會主席只好說自己不是主辦單位，不適合邀請。「政治的歸政治，體育的歸體育」的意思是政治和體育應該區別開來，運動比賽活動不應該受到政治力量的干預。由於海峽兩岸特殊的政治關係，台灣在許多領域都受到中國的打壓，類似的情況經常發生，因此「政治歸政治，X 歸 X」常見於新聞中。

> **重點詞彙 Keywords**
>
> · **歸 guī**　　　*v.*　to belong
> · **打壓 dǎiyā**　*v.*　to suppress

　　The original sentence appeared in a comment made by the spokesperson of the Presidential Office of Taiwan in 1994. At that time, the Asian Olympic Games had sent a letter inviting President Lee Teng-hui to attend the 12th Asian Games in Hiroshima, Japan, but the Chinese government later interfered. The Chinese President Jiang Zemin threatened that if President Lee attended, the Chinese team would withdraw. Later, the Kuwaiti president of the Asian Olympic Games had to say that he was not the organizer and was not suitable for the invitation. "Politics belong to politics, and sports belong to sports" means that politics and sports should be distinguished, and politics should not interfere in sports competitions. Due to the challenging political

課本沒教的台灣華語句型 50

relationship between the two sides of the Taiwan Strait, Taiwan has been suppressed by China in many areas. Similar situations occur a lot. Therefore, "zhènzhì guī zhènzhì, X guī X (Politics belong to politics; X belongs to X.)" is often seen in the news.

:: 句型 Sentence Pattern

政治（的）歸政治，N（的）＋歸＋N

:: 用法 Usage

用來描述某個領域不應該受到政治的影響。

This pattern is used to describe an area that should not be affected by politics.

:: 例句 Example

🎧 MP3-064

1 ｜ 如果真的有「政治歸政治，健康歸健康」，台灣怎麼會不能參加世界衛生組織呢？

1 ｜ If "politics belong to politics; health belongs to health" were indeed true, why can't Taiwan join the World Health Organization?

2 ｜ 說「政治歸政治，經濟歸經濟」的人並不了解政治跟經濟的關係。

2 ｜ Those who say "politics belong to politics; the economy belongs to the economy" do not understand the relationship between politics and the economy.

3 ｜ 音樂離不開生活，而生活離不開政治，那「政治歸政治，音樂歸音樂」可能嗎？

3 ｜ Music cannot be separated from life, and life cannot be separated from politics. Is it possible then for "politics belong to politics, and music belongs to music alone?"

這不是 X，什麼才是 X ？ If this is not X, what is X?

:: **原文例句 Original Sentence**　　　　　　🎧 MP3-065

這不是關說，什麼才是關說？

If this is not influence peddling, what is influence peddling?

:: **出處 Source**

　　2013 年台灣發生了一個相當於水門案的政治事件。當時的檢察總長違法監聽立法院的電話，然後告知總統馬英九，說立法院長王金平疑似司法關說。馬英九不久之後就召開記者會，斥責王金平危害司法獨立，並說出：「如果這不是關說，什麼才是關說？」既是總統也是國民黨主席的馬英九後來決定開除王金平的國民黨籍，目的是使王金平失去立法委員、院長的身分，但是王金平立即向法院提出訴訟以爭取保留黨籍資格。關說案後來經過長時間的訴訟，最終以查無事證結案，相關人都沒有被起訴，而黨籍案的訴訟，王金平也獲判勝訴而得以保持黨籍。至於檢察總長，因為對總統洩露監聽和偵辦內容，最後被判了洩密罪。

重點詞彙 Keywords

- 關說 guānshuō　　*n.*　influence peddling
- 訴訟 sùsòng　　　*n.*　lawsuit

In 2013, a political incident equivalent to the Watergate scandal occurred in Taiwan. The prosecuting Attorney General at that time illegally monitored the phone calls of the Legislative Yuan. He then informed President Ma Ying-jeou that the President of Legislative Yuan, Wang Jin-pyng, was suspected of judicial influence peddling. Ma soon held a press conference and reprimanded Wang for jeopardizing the independence of justice and said: "rúguǒ zhè bú shì guānshuō, shénme cái shì guānshuō? (If this is not influence peddling, what is influence peddling?)" Ma, who was both the President of Taiwan and Chairman of the Kuomintang (KMT), later decided to expel Wang from KMT so that Wang could lose his position as a legislator and the President of Legislative Yuan. However, Wang immediately filed a lawsuit with the court to retain his party membership. After a long period of litigation, the case was finally dismissed for insufficient evidence. No relevant people were prosecuted. In the case of party membership, Wang also won the lawsuit to keep his status. As for the prosecuting Attorney General, he was convicted of leaking secrets of surveillance and investigations to the President.

:: 句型 Sentence Pattern

1 | （如果）這不是＋ N ／ VP，什麼才是＋ (N ／ VP)？
2 | 這不是＋ N ／ VP 是什麼？

:: 用法 Usage

激問法，目的是要對方同意自己想表達的話。

This pattern is used as a rhetorical question to make the interlocutor agree with what you want to express.

:: 例句 Example

🎧 MP3-066

1 | 父母為了孩子付出那麼多，如果這不是愛，什麼才是愛？

1 | Parents give so much for their children. If it is not out of love, then what is?

2 | 報紙寫假新聞，如果這不是問題，什麼才是問題？

2 | Newspapers report fake news. If that's not a problem, what is a problem?

3 | 這個報告我已經檢查好幾次了，老闆卻還要我再檢查一次，你說這不是找麻煩是什麼？

3 | I have checked this report several times. Still, the boss wants me to check it again. If this is not picking on me, what is picking on me?

:: 原文例句 Original Sentence

🎧 MP3-067

市長我一定做好，做滿。

I promise I will fulfill my duty as mayor during my term of office.

:: 出處 Source

　　原文是出自2014年新北市長朱立倫所說的一句話。他在第二任就職的時候，承諾會把市政工作做好，並且做滿四年的市長任期，而不參選 2016 年的總統選舉。雖然朱立倫多次在訪問中提到「做好做滿」，但是到了 2015 年 10 月，國民黨卻換掉已經推出的候選人，改由朱立倫在仍然具有新北市長的身分下參選總統。那一屆總統選舉的結果是朱立倫大輸給代表民進黨的候選人蔡英文。從此「做好做滿」成為台灣社會的流行語，也是一般大眾對民選首長的基本要求。

重點詞彙 Keywords

· **市長 shìzhǎng**　　*n.*　mayor
· **選舉 xuǎnjǔ**　　*n.*　election

The original sentence was said by Chu Li-luan, the mayor of New Taipei City in 2014. When he began in his second term, he promised to do a good job for the city and to serve as mayor for a full term of four years instead of running in the 2016 presidential election. Although Chu mentioned "zuò hǎo zuò mǎn (doing a good job for the full term)" in many interviews, Kuomintang later substituted Chu for the party-nominated candidate to run in the presidential election in October 2015 while he was still the mayor of New Taipei City. The result of the election was that Chu lost to Tsai Ing-wen, the candidate of the Democratic Progressive Party, by large margin. Since then, "zuò hǎo zuò mǎn" has become a catch phrase in Taiwanese society, and "doing a good job for the full term" is also the minimum requirement that the public considers when electing a political figure.

V ＋好＋ V ＋滿

:: 用法 Usage

　　敘述徹底、充分地做某件事到滿足的程度。這個句型使用的動詞只能是單音節的。

This pattern is used to describe doing something thoroughly, fully, and to the point of satisfaction. The verbs used in this pattern can only be single syllable.

:: 例句 Example　　　　　　　　　　🎧 MP3-068

1 ｜ 下個星期開始就是百貨公司週年慶，我已經準備買好買滿了。

1 ｜ Next week begins the anniversary sales of that department store, and I am ready to buy a lot.

2 ｜ 這個皮包不但好看，而且讓你裝好裝滿，也不貴，要不要買呢？

2 ｜ This bag is not only good-looking, but also allows you to carry a lot of stuff, and it is not expensive. Do you want to buy it?

3 ｜ 現在看電視的人比以前少多了，網上什麼節目都有，大家都上網看好看滿。

3 ｜ Way fewer people watch TV now than before. There are all kinds of programs on the Internet, and everyone watches online to their heart's content.

第三單元：流行語句型

PART III: Catch Phrase Patterns

I. 流行語填空

Fill in the blanks:

> a 做好做滿 ｜ b 政治歸政治 ｜ c 寫好寫滿 ｜ d 什麼才是

1｜如果＿＿＿，電影歸電影，怎麼做電影工作的人需要說自己不想說的話呢？

2｜你要用車的時候，我就把車借給你，這不是給你方便，＿＿＿給你方便？你還有什麼不滿意的？

3｜這個工作我一定把它＿＿＿，請大家相信我，給我一個機會。

4｜體育活動大部分都需要國家的幫忙，「＿＿＿，體育歸體育」是不可能的。

5｜我讀書的習慣是把一張一張的紙＿＿＿，然後該記的就記住了。

II. 對話配對
Conversation pairing:

1 | 你已經玩了兩個小時的電
腦遊戲了，這樣對眼睛、
身體都不好，還不出去動
一動？

2 | 以前國家做錯的事，歷史
課本也應該寫。

3 | 這個週末打算做什麼呢？
我每天都給你打電話，這

4 | 不是關心，什麼才是關
心？

5 | 今天什麼問題都能問，給
大家問好問滿。

A | 我同意，應該政治歸政治，
歷史歸歷史。

B | 請問你到中國旅行的時
候，發生過什麼有趣的
事？

C | 沒別的事的話，我就去圖
書館看好看滿，那裡有書
也有電影。

D | 你只說你自己的事，那是
關心嗎？

E | 玩這個遊戲又動手又動
腳，如果這不是運動是什
麼？

▶ 挑戰你自己：用「我 X 我驕傲／政治歸政治，X 歸 X ／這不是 X，
什麼才是 X ？」完成下面的任務。
Challenge yourself: complete the task below with one of these patterns:
wǒ X wǒ jiāo'ào / zhèngzhì guī zhèngzhì, X guī X / zhè bú shì X, shénme cái
shì X?

你跟朋友打算一起去旅行，可是朋友想去的地方跟你不一樣，
你會跟他說什麼讓他同意你的計畫？

台語詞彙

　　台灣是個多語社會，除了華語以外，還使用台語、客語以及各種原住民語言。其中，台語是除了華語以外，使用人數最多的語言。不過受到 1980 年代以前的語言政策影響，會用流利台語溝通的年輕人逐年減少。因此從 2001 年開始，台灣的小學開始將本土語言納入課程中。但是無論如何，台語在台灣社會中仍是一種主流的語言。據 2009 年的研究，在台灣能使用台語的人口佔 73%。所以台灣華語不但在語法結構上受到台語的影響，在詞彙上也有許多新的台語詞彙。不過台語的詞彙要用漢字來呈現，有的用發音相近的字，有的選意思類似的詞，往往需要經過一段時間，選用的字漸漸約定俗成、穩定以後，才被大家熟知。這裡收錄了十個具有延伸性的台語詞彙，也都經常出現在日常生活與新聞媒體上。為了方便學習者識讀，詞彙標註的發音用的是中文學習者比較熟悉的漢語拼音，而不是一般台語學習者常用的台灣閩南語羅馬拼音。如果詞彙標註了台語和華語兩種發音，表示前後兩種唸法在台灣都有人說，而例句錄音採用第一種比較常聽到的台語說法。

| **PART IV** |

Taiwanese Morphemes

Taiwan is a multilingual society. Besides Mandarin, Taiwanese, Hakka, and various aboriginal languages are utilized in the society. Among all the languages, Taiwanese is the second most spoken language after Mandarin. However, having been affected by the national language policy before the 1980s, fewer young people can communicate in Taiwanese fluently now than before. Therefore, since 2001 primary schools in Taiwan began to include native languages in their curriculum. Nevertheless, Taiwanese is still a main language in Taiwan's society. According to research published in 2009, 73% of the population in Taiwan can speak Taiwanese. Hence, Táiwān Huáyǔ is not only influenced by the language Taiwanese in terms of grammatical structure, but it also adopts many Taiwanese words. However, Taiwanese vocabulary requires Chinese characters to represent it. Some have similar pronunciations, and some have similar meanings. The characters for the Taiwanese words often take time to be established and to be accepted by the public. Here are ten morphemes originating from Taiwanese, all of which often appear in daily life and news media. For the convenience of Chinese learners, the phonetic transcription of the words introduced here is Hanyu Pinyin instead of official Taiwanese Romanization, which is commonly used by Taiwanese language learners. If a word is transcribed with both Taiwanese and Mandarin pronunciations (in the order as such), it means that both pronunciations are spoken in Taiwan. In the recordings, you will hear the Taiwanese pronunciations, as they are the more commonly heard variant.

31　X 透透　X tòutòu

:: 情境例句 Contextual Example　∩ MP3-070

A：最近在忙什麼呀？好久沒看到你了。

B：為了找一把好吉他，我全台灣跑透透，看了很多家樂器行，才買到喜歡的。

A：What have you been up to lately? I haven't seen you for a long time.

B：For finding a good guitar, I ran all over Taiwan and checked out many musical instrument stores until I bought the one I like.

:: 結構說明 Structure

　　X 透透：「透透（tòutòu）」是到處或者徹底的意思，X 可以代入走、跑、吃、玩等單音節的動作動詞，和「透透」合在一起分別是到處走、到處跑、買很多不同種類的東西、吃很多不同種類的東西、到處玩。X 透透前一般有一個地方詞，表示活動在這個地方的範圍內進行。

　　X tòutòu: "tòutòu 'thoroughly'" means to go around or do something thoroughly. X can be single-syllable action verbs such as zǒu 'walk', pǎo 'run', mǎi 'buy', chī 'eat', wán 'play', etc. Those verbs combining with "tòutòu" mean to go around, run around, buy many different kinds of things, eat many different kinds of foods, play around respectively. "X tòutòu" is generally preceded by a locative noun to indicate that the activity is within the place.

:: 合成詞與例句 Example　∩ MP3-071

1 | **跑透透**
我女兒台北跑透透就為了寫歷史課的作業。看，她變得這麼黑。

1 | **pǎo tòutòu**
My daughter ran around Taipei just to write history class homework. See, she became so tanned.

2 | 走透透

大學畢業以後我就在航空公司工作，所以可以全世界走透透。

2 | zǒu tòutòu

After graduating from university, I worked at an airline, so I could travel all over the world.

3 | 買透透

下個月要不要跟我去東京買透透、玩透透啊？

3 | mǎi tòutòu

Would you like to go to Tokyo with me next month to go crazy shopping and playing?

4 | 吃透透

阿元才到台灣半年，已經台灣夜市吃透透了，你怎麼到現在還沒吃過牛肉麵？

4 | chī tòutòu

A Yuan has been in Taiwan for half a year and has already eaten his way through the night markets in Taiwan. How come you still haven't eaten beef noodles until now?

！你知道嗎 Do you know

「走」在古代漢語中是「跑」的意思，這樣的用法還保留在台語／閩南語中，因此「跑透透」和「走透透」可以說是同義詞，都是在某個地方範圍內到處奔波。另一個跟「走」相關的常用詞是「趴趴走（pāpāzào／pāpāzǒu）」意思是到處亂走但不限在一個範圍，例句：「你一天到晚趴趴走，我都找不到你。」

The word "zǒu" has a sense of "run" in classical Chinese, and this usage is retained in Taiwanese / Hokkien, so "pǎo tòutòu (run around)" and "zǒu tòutòu (walk / run around)" can be synonymous. Both mean to run around but confined to a place. A word related to "zǒu" is "pāpāzǒu / pāpāzào" which means to run around but NOT restricted to a place, e.g., "Nǐ yì tiān dào wǎn pāpāzǒu, wǒ dōu zhǎo bú dào nǐ. (You're always out running around all the time. I can never find you.)"

32 | X 步 X bō / bù

:: 情境例句 Contextual Example　　🎧 MP3-072

A：為什麼你煮的飯特別好吃呢？

B：因為有人教過我幾個小撇步啊。你也想學嗎？

A：Why is the rice you cook so tasty?

B：Because someone taught me a few tips. Do you want to learn too?

:: 結構說明 Structure

　　X 步：「步（bō / bù）」是手段、方法的意思，X 可以代入奧（ào）、撇（piě）。「奧步」指的是卑劣的手段，「撇步」指的是好方法或捷徑。

　　　X bù: "bō / bù 'step'" means approach or method. X can be ào 'bad' and phiet / piě. "àobō / àobù" is despicable means, and "phietbō / piěbù" is good method or shortcuts.

:: 合成詞與例句 Example　　🎧 MP3-073

1 | 撇步

想學好語言沒有什麼撇步，就是要天天練習。

1 | phietbō / piěbù

There is no shortcut to learning a language well. It's all about practicing every day.

2 | 奧步

我就是輸，也不會用奧步去贏得比賽。

2 | àobō / àobù

Even if I am losing, I will not use dirty tricks to win a race.

! 原來如此 No Wonder

下棋的時候，每一次移動一次棋子，叫做「一步」。下棋的目的是贏對方，因此每一步都是為了打贏對方而採取的動作，所以下棋的「步」引申有「手段、方法」的意思。「撇步」的「撇」在台語中是「走路時腳向外偏斜、非正規」的意思，所以「撇步」有好方法或高明的手段的意思。

When playing chess, every move is called "yí bù (one step)." The purpose of playing chess is to defeat the opponent. Each move is an action taken to beat the opponent, so the word "bù" in chess has the connotation of "means and method." "phiet / piě" in "phietbō / piěbù" has the sense of "walking with feet outwardly and inclined, i.e., irregularly" in Taiwanese, so "piěbù" means a good method or a brilliant approach.

:: **情境例句 Contextual Example**　　🎧 MP3-074

A：他們不是最強的嗎？怎麼輸了
　　呢？

B：唉，對手用了奧步，又沒有被
　　抓到，最後就這樣了。

A：Aren't they the strongest? How did
　　they lose?

B：Sigh. The opponent used dirty tricks
　　and did not get caught. That was the
　　end of it.

:: **結構說明 Structure**

　　奧 X：「奧（ào）」這裡是惡劣的意思，X 可以代入步、客。「奧步」的意思是卑劣的手段，「奧客」是指很會找商家麻煩、難以對付的客人。

　　ào X: "ào" here means bad. X can be bù 'step' or kè 'customer'. "àobō / àobù" means despicable tactics, and "àokeh / àokè" means a customer who is very troublesome and difficult to deal with.

:: **合成詞與例句 Example**　　🎧 MP3-075

1 | **奧步**

他們公司用了奧步才得到那筆
生意。

1 | **àobō / àobù**

Their company used dirty trick to get
the deal.

2 | **奧客**

今天來了一個奧客，說他的麵
裡有髒東西，又不付錢，我只
好打電話叫警察。

2 | **àokeh / àokè**

Today there was a difficult customer
who said something dirty was in his
noodles, and he didn't want to pay,
so I had to call the police.

課本沒教的台灣華語句型50

！原來如此 No Wonder

　　「奧（ào）」這個發音的正規台語文字寫作「漚」，是指蔬菜水果腐爛或是不新鮮、有臭味，也用來形容爛的、不好的或卑劣的人事物。2007 年到 2008 年之間，「奧步」這個詞大量出現在台灣的政治新聞裡，因為當時正在進行總統大選，各陣營的政治人物時常指責對手使用奧步，像是醜化對方或者散播不實的謠言，也就是所謂的「抹黑（mǒhēi）」對手。

"ào" is formally written as "漚" in Taiwanese. It refers to rotten, stale, smelly vegetables and fruits. It is also used to describe rotten, bad, or despicable people and things. Between 2007 and 2008, the word "àobō / àobù" appeared in Taiwan's political news a lot because the presidential election was on-going at that time, and politicians from different camps often accused opponents of using àobō / àobù, like demonizing the opponent or spreading false rumors. That is so-called "mǒhēi (smearing)" an opponent.

II. 填空

Fill in the blank:

> a 奧步 ｜ b 跑透透 ｜ c 撇步 ｜ d 吃透透 ｜ e 奧客

1｜為什麼這些花開得那麼漂亮？你有什麼 ＿＿＿ 嗎？

2｜開店一年多還沒見過像她那樣的 ＿＿＿，衣服已經穿過幾次了還想要換新的。

3｜新工作需要我全台灣 ＿＿＿，累死了！

4｜阿海用了 ＿＿＿ 才得到那個獎，他的成績並沒有好到可以得到那個獎。

5｜你來台灣找我，我帶你全台美食 ＿＿＿。

II. 選出適合的交談對話內容：

Choose the appropriate conversation content:

（　　）1｜A：你的漢字寫得真好看。

　　　　　　B：❶ 哪裡哪裡，沒什麼撇步，就是每天練習。

　　　　　　　　❷ 用了奧步才變成這樣。

（　　）2｜A：寒假放四個星期，好無聊喔。

　　　　　　B：❶ 你用奧步！可以這樣嗎？

　　　　　　　　❷ 帶你去台中玩透透怎麼樣？

（　　）3｜A：這雙鞋那個人已經換了五次了，還不滿意，今天又拿來換了。

　　　　　　B：❶ 又來一個奧客啊？

　　　　　　　　❷ 快來買透透吧。

（　）4｜A：在你的國家，人們擔心 Covid-19 嗎？

　　　　B：❶ 大家還是都趴趴走，都沒在怕的。

　　　　　　❷ 我有不生病的撇步。

（　）5｜A：老闆沒讓你當美國公司的經理，是因為阿中跟很多人說你
　　　　　　不喜歡坐飛機。

　　　　B：❶ 他自己去美國吃透透了。

　　　　　　❷ 這是什麼奧步？

▶ 挑戰你自己：用「X 透透／X 步／奧 X」延伸上面任何一個對話。

Challenge yourself: Use X tòutòu / X bō / ào X to extend any of the dialogues above.

:: **情境例句 Contextual Example**　　🎧 MP3-077

A：這個演員努力了十幾年才從 C 咖變成大咖。

B：是啊，真不容易。

A：This actor has worked hard for more than ten years to become a big star from a small potato.

B：Yeah, it's really not easy.

:: **結構說明 Structure**

　　X 咖：「咖（kā）」是角色或人物的意思，X 可以代入大、小、A、B、C、怪、爛等，表示角色的重要程度或對某個人的評價，「大咖」、「A 咖」都是指重要的角色，「B 咖」、「C 咖」依序次之，和「小咖」一樣，都是比較不重要的人。「怪咖」是指奇怪的人，「爛咖」是指糟糕的人。

　　X kā: "kā" means role or character. X can be dà 'big', xiǎo 'small', A, B, C, guài 'odd', làn 'rotten', etc. It indicates how important the role is or talks about the judgement about a certain person. "dàkā" and "A kā" both refer to important roles. "B kā" and "C kā" are the next in order! They are the same as "xiǎokā," meaning less important roles. "guàikā" refers to quirky people, and "lànkā" refers to lousy people.

:: **合成詞與例句 Example**　　🎧 MP3-078

1 | **A 咖**

這個計畫這麼重要，我們當然要找公司裡的 A 咖去參加會議。

1 | **A kā**

The project is so important that we sure need to get the A-listers from the company to attend the meeting.

2 | **小咖**

老闆真的要我去嗎？我這麼小咖能做決定嗎？

2 | **xiǎokā**

Does the boss really want me to go? Can a small potato like me make a decision?

3 | 怪咖

我有一個怪咖同事，一到辦公室就睡覺，總要等到有電話進來，才開始工作。但是工作成績不錯，大家也就沒說什麼。

3 | guàikā

I have a quirky colleague. He sleeps when he arrives at the office and never works until a phone call comes in. But he doesn't do his job badly, so people do not say anything about him.

4 | 爛咖

什麼！他有四個女朋友？真是個爛咖！

4 | lànkā

What! He has four girlfriends? What scum!

！你知道嗎 Do you know

　　台語「咖」除了「角色」的意思，還有夥伴、或是某個群體中的一份子的意思，例如跟你一起打牌或打麻將的人就是你的「牌咖」。「咖」與台語的「腳（kā）」同音，「柱仔腳（tiáo a kā）」，或華語的「椿腳（zhuāngjiǎo）」是台灣社會裡一種特定的角色，是在選舉期間經常出現的詞彙，指的是在選舉中對候選人很重要的主要支持者，並且對地方政治非常熟悉，也有一定影響力。

In addition to the sense of "role", "kā" in Taiwanese also has a sense of "partner" or "a member of a group." For example, people who play cards or mahjong with you are called your "páikā." "kā" has a homophone in Taiwanese meaning "foot." "tiáo a kā", or "zhuāngjiǎo" in Mandarin, has a specific role in Taiwan's society. This word often appears a lot during elections, refers to a major supporter who is important to a candidate in an election, and is familiar with local politics and is influential among the public.

:: 情境例句 Contextual Example 🎧 MP3-079

A：上個星期買的新手機怎麼樣？

B：不錯用，比舊的方便多了。

A： How is the new cell phone you bought last week?

B： Not bad, much more convenient than the old one.

:: 結構說明 Structure

不錯 X：「不錯（búcuò）」就是好的意思，X 可以代入吃、喝、看、聽、用等單音節的動詞，和「不錯」合起來的意思分別相當於好吃、好喝、好看、好聽、好用。

búcuò X: "búcuò" means good. X can be single-syllable verb, such as chī 'eat', hē 'drink', kàn 'see', tīng 'listen', and yòng 'use', which combine with búcuò meaning good to eat / tasty, good to drink, good to see / pretty, good to listen, and good to use respectively.

:: 合成詞與例句 Example 🎧 MP3-080

1 | **不錯吃**

這家餐廳的蘋果蛋糕不錯吃喔，你要不要試看看？

1 | **búcuò chī**

The apple cake at this restaurant is tasty. Would you like to try it?

2 | **不錯喝**

我覺得這種咖啡不錯喝，可是有一點貴。

2 | **búcuò hē**

I think this kind of coffee is good, but it's a bit expensive.

3 | **不錯看**

你的新鞋子不錯看，在哪裡買的啊？

3 | **búcuò kàn**

Your new shoes look nice. Where did you buy them?

4 | 不錯聽

昨天電影的音樂不錯聽，你知道是誰做的嗎？

4 | búcuò tīng

The music in yesterday's movie was good. Do you know who composed it?

! 你知道嗎 Do you know

　　雖然「不錯 X」相當於「好 X」，但不是每一個「好 X」都可以替換成「不錯 X」，例如「這雙鞋很好走」的「好走」並不能代換成「* 不錯走」。目前使用頻率比較高的只侷限在單音節的感官動詞「吃、喝、看、聽」，以及「用、玩」。

　　Although "búcuò X" is equivalent to "hǎo X (good to X)", not every "hǎo X" can be replaced with "búcuò X." For example, "hǎo zǒu 'good to walk'" in "zhè shuāng xié hěn hǎo zǒu. (This pair of shoes is easy to walk in.)" cannot be replaced by " *búcuò zǒu." Currently, the most frequently used verbs are limited to single-syllable sensory verbs, such as chī 'eat', hē 'drink', kàn 'see', and tīng 'listen', plus yòng 'use' and wán 'play'.

:: 情境例句 Contextual Example　　　∩ MP3-081

A：今天有夠熱的。

B：去洗個冷水澡就會好一點了。

A：It's so hot today.

B：Go take a cold shower and you will feel better.

:: 結構說明 Structure

　　有夠 X：「有夠（yǒugòu）」是真的很……的意思，X 可以代入重、漂亮、簡單、麻煩……等等狀態動詞，和「有夠」合起來的意思分別是真的很重、真的很漂亮、真的很簡單、真的很麻煩。「有夠 X」經常用在抱怨或讚美的時候。

yǒugòu X: "yǒugòu" means really…. X can be zhòng 'heavy', piàoliàng 'beautiful', jiǎndān 'simple', máfán 'troublesome', etc., which combine with yǒugòu meaning really heavy, really pretty, really simple, and really troublesome respectively. "yǒugòu X" is often used when complaining or praising.

:: 合成詞與例句 Example　　　∩ MP3-082

1 | **有夠重**

你的行李有夠重，這裡面你裝了什麼啊？

1 | **yǒugòu zhòng**

Your luggage is so heavy. What did you pack in it?

2 | **有夠漂亮**

台灣東部的海有夠漂亮，你一定要去看看。

2 | **yǒugòu piàoliàng**

The sea by eastern Taiwan is so beautiful. You must go visit.

3 | **有夠簡單**

今天上午的數學考試有夠簡單，不到半個小時我就寫完了。

3 | **yǒugòu jiǎndān**

The math test this morning was so easy. I finished it in less than half an hour.

4 | 有夠麻煩

華人文化中送禮物有很多要注意的事情，有夠麻煩的。

4 | yǒugòu máfán

There is so much etiquette you should pay attention to when giving gifts in Chinese culture. It is so troublesome.

！你知道嗎 Do you know

在華語中，「夠」的意思是達到一定的量，例如：「這些菜夠六個人吃了。」「這點錢不夠買一台電腦。」如果「夠」的後面接狀態動詞，意思就是某種狀態達到一個讓人滿足的程度，例如：「夠認真」、「夠勇敢」、「老師上課的聲音不夠大聲，我聽得很辛苦。」「有夠」雖然是從台語來的，其中的「夠」也和華語的一樣，是指某種狀態達滿足程度的意思，而「有夠」是說話者覺得某人、事或物真的很怎麼樣，十分值得聽話者注意。

In Mandarin, "gòu 'enough'" has a sense of reaching to a certain amount, e.g., "Zhè xiē cài gòu liù ge rén chī le. (These dishes are enough for six people.)" "Zhè diǎn qián bú gòu mǎi yì tái diànnǎo. (This is not enough money to buy a computer.)" If "gòu" is followed by a stative verb, it means that a certain state of being has reached a level of satisfaction, e.g., gòu rènzhēn (hardworking enough), gòu yǒnggǎn (brave enough), and "Lǎoshī shàngkè de shēngyīn bú gòu dà, wǒ tīng de hěn xīnkǔ. (The teacher's voice is not loud enough for the class. I have a hard time hearing her.)" Although the word "yǒu gòu" originates from Taiwanese, gòu, which carries the same sense as in Mandarin, also means that a certain state of being has reached a level of satisfaction. By saying "yǒugòu", a speaker expresses someone or something (including physical and non-physical), is really noticeable and deserves the listener's attention.

I. 填空
Fill in the blank:

> a 不錯看 ｜ b A咖 ｜ c 有夠好吃 ｜ d 不錯用 ｜ e 小咖

1｜昨天那家餐廳的菜 _____，又不貴，我們星期五再去一次吧。

2｜他已經老了嗎？以前都是他打得最好，現在一個 _____ 也能打贏他。

3｜聽說那種洗衣機 _____，不需要很多水就可以把衣服洗得非常乾淨。

4｜這件毛衣 _____，在哪裡買的？

5｜幾年不見她已經變成 _____ 了，現在忙得很，要約她見面很難了。

II. 選出適合的交談對話內容：
Choose the appropriate conversation content:

（　　）1｜A：這次的活動，公司只打算花十萬塊。

　　　　　　B：❶ 我有去，東西都不錯吃。

　　　　　　　　❷ 錢這麼少，請得到大咖嗎？

（　　）2｜A：❶ 怎麼有人把車停在門口？讓我有夠生氣的。

　　　　　　　　❷ 台北動物園真的不錯玩。

　　　　　　B：打電話給警察啊。

（　　）3｜A：我昨天看到小美現在的男朋友跟別的女人在一起。

　　　　　　B：❶ 為什麼小美總是喜歡爛咖呢？

　　　　　　　　❷ 小美今天有夠漂亮的。

（　　）4｜A：❶ 這種果汁不錯喝，你要不要喝看看？

　　　　　　　　❷ 上午的考試有夠難，你覺得呢？

　　　　　　B：好啊，給我一些試試。

（　　）5｜A：星期五下班以後，我們去 KTV 怎麼樣？

B：❶ 我不要跟怪咖在一起。

❷ 阿明唱歌不錯聽，找他一起去。

▶ 挑戰你自己：用「X 咖／不錯 X ／有夠 X」延伸上面任何一個對話。

Challenge yourself: Use X kā / búcuò X / yǒugòu X to extend any of the dialogues above.

:: 情境例句 Contextual Example　🎧 MP3-084

A：這照片你拍的嗎？好美啊。

B：沒什麼啦，我黑白拍的。

A：Did you take this photo? It's so beautiful.

B：That's nothing. I just snapped casually.

:: 結構說明 Structure

　　黑白 X：「黑白（hēibái）」是隨便、不認真或沒有用心，也就是胡亂的意思，X 可以代入講、買、賣、寫等常用的單音節動作動詞，和「黑白」合起來分別是胡亂講、胡亂買、胡亂賣、胡亂寫。

　　hēibái X: "hēibái 'black-white'" has a sense of casual, not serious or inattentive, i.e., indiscriminately. X can be common monosyllabic verbs, such as jiǎng 'speak', mǎi 'buy', mài 'sell', xiě 'write', etc., and combine with hēibái to mean talk carelessly, shop carelessly, sell carelessly, write carelessly respectively.

:: 合成詞與例句 Example　🎧 MP3-085

1 | **黑白講**
感冒可以喝可樂當藥？你不要黑白講！

1 | **hēibái jiǎng**
I can drink cola as medicine for a cold? Don't talk nonsense!

2 | **黑白買**
我妹妹常常黑白買，家裡好多沒有用的東西。

2 | **hēibái mǎi**
My younger sister often shops impulsively. A lot of useless things pile up at home.

3 | **黑白賣**
來來來！今天老闆不在，黑白賣，買一送一，買到賺到。

3 | **hēibái mài**
Come on! Today the boss is not here. Sale frenzy. Buy one get one free. You buy and you earn.

4 | **黑白寫**

今天的考試真難，我只好黑白寫。

4 | **hēibái xiě**

Today's exam is so hard. I have no choice but to scribble.

！你知道嗎 Do you know

　　表達不用心或胡亂做某一件事的時候，除了台語來的「黑白X」，也可以用華語的「隨便X」或者「亂X」，例如：「隨便吃、隨便畫、亂買、亂看」。不過「隨便X」還有另外一個意思是沒有拘束、隨心意去做某事，例如：「不好意思，家裡有點亂，請隨便坐。」

When expressing carelessness or doing something indiscriminately, you can also use "suíbiàn X" or "luàn X" in Mandarin besides "hēibái X", such as suíbiàn chī (eat indiscriminately), suíbiàn huà (scribble), luàn mǎi (shopping spree), and luàn kàn (snoop around). However, "suíbiàn X" also has another sense that is to be unrestrained and do something as you like. For example, "Bùhǎoyìsi, jiā lǐ yǒu diǎn luàn, qǐng suíbiàn zuò. (I am sorry. The house is a little messy. Please sit anywhere you like.)"

38

加減 X jiājiǎn X

:: **情境例句 Contextual Example**　　　∩ MP3-086

A：我現在不舒服，不想吃東西。

B：不行，不吃的話，病不會好。
　　加減吃一點吧。

A：I am not feeling well now and do not
　　want to eat.

B：No, if you don't eat, you won't get
　　well. Eat some more or less.

:: **結構說明 Structure**

　　加減 X：「加減 (jiājiǎn)」是或多或少的意思，X 可以代入看、讀、學、運動等常用動作動詞，和「加減」合在一起分別是多多少少看一些、多多少少讀一些、多多少少學一些、多多少少運動一點。「加減 X」後面經常搭配一些、一點、一下等表示量少的詞，或者把動詞 X 重疊來表示動作的量少，例如：「加減看看」。

　　jiājiǎn X: "jiājiǎn 'addition-subtraction'" means more or less. X can be common action verbs, such as kàn 'see', dú 'read', xué 'learn', yùndòng 'exercise', etc. They combine with "jiājiǎn" to mean read more or less, study more or less, learn more or less, and exercise more or less respectively. The word following jiājiǎn X is that indicates a small amount, such as "yìxiē 'some', yìdiǎn 'a little bit', yíxià 'once',", or duplicates the verb X to get the sense of small quantity in action, e.g., "jiājiǎn kànkan (take a look more or less)."

:: **合成詞與例句 Example**　　　∩ MP3-087

1 | **加減看**
　　沒有買沒關係，加減看看。

1 | **jiājiǎn kàn**
　　It doesn't matter if you don't buy it.
　　Just take a look.

2 | **加減讀**
　　明天就要考試了，還有這麼多
　　沒念完，現在只能加減讀一
　　些。

2 | **jiājiǎn dú**
　　The exam is coming tomorrow. I still
　　have so many pages not studied.
　　Now I can only study some.

3 | **加減學**

看美國電影可以加減學一點英文。

3 | **jiājiǎn xué**

You can learn English more or less by watching American movies.

4 | **加減運動**

我們吃完晚餐去走一走，加減運動一下。

4 | **jiājiǎn yùndòng**

Let's take a walk after dinner and exercise more or less.

！**原來如此** No wonder

　　「加減 X」經常使用在建議別人做某事，在動詞 X 後面接表示量少的詞，有讓對方輕鬆一點、不太費力地試試看的意思。「加減」也可以替換其他表示量少的詞，像是「稍微、稍稍、多少、多多少少」，例如：「雖然天氣很冷，但是身體還是應該多少動一動。」

　　"jiājiǎn X" is often used to advise someone to do something, and the verb is followed by a word that indicates a small amount. This makes the suggestion sound easier for the interlocutor to attempt with less effort. "jiājiǎn" can be replaced with the word that has the sense of small quantity, such as "shāowēi 'a little', shāoshāo 'a little', duōshǎo, and duōduōshǎoshǎo (both meaning more or less)." For example, "Suīrán tiānqì hěn lěng, dànshì shēngtǐ háishì yīnggāi duōshǎo dòng yí dòng. (Although it's cold, you should move your body a little bit.)"

39 X 衰 X suēi / shuāi

:: 情境例句 Contextual Example　　🎧 MP3-088

A：哥哥要 90 公斤瘦到 75 公斤，
　　我看是不可能的啦。

B：他那麼努力，你不要唱衰他！

A：My elder brother wants to lose
　　weight from 90 kg to 75 kg. I think it
　　is impossible.

B：He worked so hard. Don't talk him
　　down.

:: 結構說明 Structure

　　X 衰：「衰（suēi / shuāi）」是倒楣、運氣不好的意思，X 可以代入看、唱、
帶。「看衰」是看壞，不認為某事會成功或順利。「唱衰」是說出不看好的話，
也是希望某事不會成功或不順利。「帶衰」是使別人跟著倒楣，或是某事因而
不成功。

　　X suēi: "suēi" has a sense of bad luck or unlucky. X can be kàn 'see', chàng 'sing',
and dài 'bring'. "kànsuēi" means not optimistic toward something, or not thinking
that something will succeed or go well. "chàngsuēi" is to say something that is
not optimistic, also hoping that something will not succeed or go well. "dàisuēi" is
someone bringing bad luck to others, or making something unsuccessful because of
him / her.

:: 合成詞與例句 Example　　🎧 MP3-089

1 | **看衰**
　　這家公司生意做得非常好，沒
　　有人看衰他們明年開新公司的
　　計畫。

1 | **kànsuēi / kànshuāi**
　　This company's business is doing
　　very well, and no one looks down
　　on their plans to open a new branch
　　next year.

2 | 唱衰

很多人唱衰阿明，說他參加游泳比賽一定會是最後一名，想不到他得到第一名。

2 | chàngsuēi / chàngshuāi

Many people bad-mouthed A Ming, saying that he would definitely come in last in the swimming competition, but unexpectedly he got first place.

3 | 帶衰

我這個星期不是找不到東西，就是被老闆不停的丟工作，不知道被誰帶衰了？

3 | dàisuēi / dàishuāi

This week, I either couldn't find anything, or constantly had assignments dumped on me by my boss. I wonder who caused me the bad luck?

！你知道嗎 Do you know

「唱衰」只是用言語詛咒別人不能成功，而要是一個人「看衰」或「帶衰」別人，他並沒有做出實際的行動致使別人不成功。如果有人付諸實際行動，對別人的行動加以破壞、阻擾，以致於別人不能達到期望的目的，這樣的行為叫做「扯後腿」，例如：「我們這次的計畫又沒成功，一定是有人扯後腿。」

"chàngsuēi" is just cursing others with words for not succeeding. If a person "chàngsuēi" or "dàisuēi" others, he/she does not take actual actions to make others unsuccessful. When someone puts into practice disrupting or obstructing of the actions of others so that they cannot achieve the desired goal, such behavior is called "chě hòutuǐ 'pull the hind legs'", e.g., "Wǒmen zhè cì de jìhuà yòu méi chénggōng, yídìng shì yǒu rén chě hòutuǐ. (Our plan failed again this time. There must be someone holding us back.)"

:: **情境例句 Contextual Example**　　🎧 MP3-090

A：他跑攤是喝了幾杯啊？怎麼臉那麼紅？

B：我看喝得不少喔。

A：How many glasses did he drink while bar hopping? Why is his face so flushed?

B：I think he drank a lot.

:: **結構說明 Structure**

　　X 攤：「攤（tuān / tān）」是飯局的意思，也是計算飯局的單位，X 可以代入跑、趕、續。「跑攤」是指政治人物去參加很多有群眾聚會的活動。「趕攤」是趕著去參加飯局。「續攤」是指在一個地方玩樂以後，再去下一個地方繼續玩樂。

　　X tuān: "tuān / tān" has a sense of a feast. It is also used as the unit for counting a feast. X can be pǎo 'run', gǎn 'rush', and xù 'continue'. "pǎo tuān / pǎo tān" refers to a politician who goes to many activities with mass gatherings. "gǎn tuān / gǎn tān" is to rush to a feast. "xù tuān / xù tān" refers to having fun in one place, and then going to the next place to continue having fun.

:: **合成詞與例句 Example**　　🎧 MP3-091

1｜**跑攤**

不好意思，我要先走了，我還要跑攤。

1｜**pǎo tuān / pǎo tān**

Sorry, I am going to take off. I have another gathering to run to.

2｜**趕攤**

我今天要早一點下班，晚上趕攤，朋友生日。

2｜**gǎn tuān / gǎn tān**

Today I need to leave work a little earlier. I have to rush to a gathering this evening for my friend's birthday.

3 | 續攤

這裡結束以後，大家還想去哪裡續攤啊？

3 | xù tuān / xù tān

After this is over, where else do you all want to go?

！原來如此 No wonder

「攤」的中文發音是 tān，當名詞用，是指擺出東西販賣的地方，例如「地攤」、「小攤子」。「X 攤」tuān 是台語的發音。在台灣，政治人物經常出席廟會慶典、節日活動、結婚、出殯等有很多人聚集的場合來增加曝光度，進而爭取民眾的支持以獲得選票。他們有的時候一天需要出席很多「攤」，所以需要跑攤、趕攤，形成台灣特殊的「跑攤文化」。現在即使不是政治人物也會使用「跑攤、「趕攤」來描述參加飯局。

The pronunciation of " 攤 " in Mandarin is tān. When it is used as a noun, it refers to a market stall, such as "dìtān (street stall)" and "xiǎotān (small stall)." "X tuān" is the Taiwanese pronunciation. In Taiwan, politicians often attend temple fairs, festivals, marriages, funerals, and other occasions where many people gather to increase exposure and then earn the support of the people to get votes. Sometimes they need to attend many "tuān" a day, so they need to run or rush there. It becomes Taiwan's special "pǎo tuān" culture. Now, even if you are not a politician, you can also use "pǎo tuān" and "gǎn tuān" to describe party hopping.

I. 填空
Fill in the blank:

> a 加減吃 | b 看衰 | c 黑白講 | d 跑攤 | e 加減買

1 | 張經理唱歌很好聽。＿＿＿＿的時候，總是有人要他唱歌。明天我們也可以找他唱歌。

2 | 快過年了，餅乾、糖果＿＿＿＿一些，請客人吃。

3 | 以前很多人都＿＿＿＿他，沒想到他現在變成了大咖。

4 | 誰說他是用奧步贏的？別＿＿＿＿了。

5 | 別人做飯請你吃，要是不好吃也要＿＿＿＿一點，這樣才有禮貌。

II. 選出適合的交談對話內容：
Choose the appropriate conversation content:

（　　）1 | A：❶ 是誰這麼壞，在牆上黑白畫？

　　　　　　❷ 等一下就要交了，加減畫一下吧。

　　　　B：一定是附近的小孩。不知道洗不洗得掉？

（　　）2 | A：你不是才剛來沒多久嗎？怎麼現在要走了呢？

　　　　B：❶ 你總是唱衰他，他怎麼會想來呢？

　　　　　　❷ 不好意思，我還要趕攤，下次再跟你喝一杯。

（　　）3 | A：大明跟阿美下個月要結婚了。

　　　　B：❶ 你別黑白看了，快認真工作。

　　　　　　❷ 是嗎？很多人看衰他們的。

（　　）4 | A：你花那麼多錢和時間上書法課，學得怎麼樣了？

　　　　B：❶ 加減學了一點，還要多練習啦。

　　　　　　❷ 我這麼努力才不怕被帶衰呢。

（　）5｜A：這是最後一個菜了，可是好像沒吃到什麼。

B：❶ 時間還早，那我們去哪裡續攤？

❷ 我昨天黑白吃，現在還肚子痛。

▶ 挑戰你自己：用「黑白 X ／加減 X ／ X 衰／ X 攤」延伸上面任何一個對話。

Challenge yourself: Use hēibái X / jiājiǎn X / X suēi / X tuān to extend any of the dialogues above.

第四單元：台語詞彙

PART IV: Taiwanese morphemes

外來語詞彙

　　外來語源自外國語言，是隨著新的事物或是概念傳入的。在台灣華語中，有的外來語，特別是來自英語的，直接使用外語的語音與字母，例如：QR Code、LED、USB；有的轉換成在地的語文輸入，然後慢慢地在地化，經過一段時間以後又再經歷不同程度的創新，使得這些外來語演化成和原本的外國語不完全相同的意思，以及不完全相同的社會觀感，原來也許帶有負面涵意，可能不再存在了。台灣華語的外來語大多來自英語和日語，顯示外國訊息來源以及文化交流以美國和日本為主。另外，日本也使用漢字，有些漢字詞的語意與中文相同或相近，因此來自日語的外來語比較容易被華語圈的使用者理解並且接受。這裡收集了十個有衍生性的外來語詞彙，其中，第 41-45 個詞彙是從英語來的，第46-50 個詞彙是從日語來的。這些外來語的使用並不侷限於台灣，在中國也是很常見的。

Loan Morphemes

Loan words are derived from foreign languages and are introduced into their new language through new things or concepts. In Táiwān Huáyǔ, some loan words, especially those from English, are directly adopted with their foreign language pronunciation and spelling, such as QR Code, LED, USB, and some are converted into the local language to be adopted and then slowly localized after a period of time. Later, these localized words go through different degrees of innovation and generate new connotations that are not exactly the same as the original foreign language and social perception. Some of them may originally have negative connotations but no longer do. Most of the loan words in Táiwān Huáyǔ come from English and Japanese, indicating that the sources of foreign information and culture are mainly from the United States and Japan. In addition, Japan also uses Chinese characters (kanji). Because some of the words written in Japanese kanji are of the same or similar meaning to Chinese, the words are easier to understand and are more readily accepted by users in the Chinese language-speaking community. Here is a collection of ten derivative loan morphemes. 41-45 are from English, and 46-50 are from Japanese. The use of these loan words is not limited to Taiwan but also very common in China.

XX 粉 XX fěn

:: 情境例句 Contextual Example

🎧 MP3-093

A：我弟弟是超級果粉，手機、電腦都要買蘋果的。

B：我也是果粉耶！

A：My younger brother is a super Apple fan. Cell phone and computer, he must buy Apple's.

B：I am an Apple fan too!

:: 結構說明 Structure

XX 粉：「粉（fěn）」或是「粉絲（fěnsī）」是英文「fans」的音譯，「粉絲」原來指的是喜愛某位藝人的影迷或是歌迷，後來也用「XX 粉」指的是喜愛某種東西或人物的人，XX 可以代入各種商品的名稱，例如「果粉」指的是喜歡蘋果（Apple）商品的人，也可以代入某人名字的一部分，例如「英粉」是蔡英文總統的忠實支持者。另外，「鐵粉」是指最忠誠的粉絲，「圈粉」是指吸引別人，讓人變成某粉絲。

XX fěn: "fěn" or "fěnsī" is transliterated from the English word "fans." "fěnsī" originally refers to fans who love an artist in show business. Later, "XX fěn" is also used to refer to a person who likes a certain thing or someone. XX can be the names of various products. For example, "guǒfěn" refers to people who like Apple products as Apple is pínguǒ in Mandarin. It can also be a part of someone's name. For example, "yīngfěn" refers to a loyal supporter of President Tsai Ing-wen. In addition, "tiěfěn" refers to loyal fans as tiě means "iron" in Mandarin. "quān fěn" refers to attracting others and turning people into a fan of some sort as quān means "enclose" in Mandarin.

1 ｜ **粉絲**

他對粉絲非常好，還常常辦只有自己的粉絲才能參加的活動。你想不到吧？

1 ｜ **fěnsī**

He treats his fans very nicely, and often holds exclusive events for them. You wouldn't expect that, would you?

2 ｜ **鐵粉**

我是費德勒 (Roger Federer) 的鐵粉，有他的比賽，我都要看！

2 ｜ **tiěfěn**

I am Roger Federer's loyal fan. Whenever he has a game, I must watch it.

3 ｜ **圈粉**

費德勒這一球打得太漂亮了，我被圈粉了。

3 ｜ **quān fěn**

Federer hit this shot so beautifully. I became his fan.

❗ **你知道嗎 Do you know**

在「粉絲」這個詞出現以前，中文也用「XX 迷（mí）」來指喜愛某種事物或某個影視歌星名人的人。相較於「果粉、英粉」等，在「粉」的前面接的是特定、明確的名詞，「迷」的前面接的是一般名詞，常見的有：棒球迷、影迷、歌迷，也有喜歡火車相關事物的「火車迷／鐵道迷」，喜歡看美國電視劇的「美劇迷」等等。流行語「黑粉」指的是惡意抹黑批評某名人的粉絲。

Before the word "fěnsī" appeared, "XX mí" was the only word used to refer to people who liked something or a celebrity in show business. Compared with guǒfěn and yīngfěn, the preceding nouns of fěn are specific; while the preceding nouns of mí are generic. The common ones are: bàngqiúmí (baseball fan), yǐngmí (movie fan), gēmí (singer's fan), as well as "huǒchēmí / tiědàomí," who love train-related things and "měijùmí (American drama fans)," who love to watch American dramas. The buzzword "hēifěn" refers to fans who maliciously slander and criticize a celebrity.

:: 情境例句 Contextual Example　　　🎧 MP3-095

A：明天晚上有一個煙火秀，你想　　　A：There is a fireworks show tomorrow
　　不想去看？　　　　　　　　　　　　 evening. Would you like to watch it?

B：好啊，在哪裡？　　　　　　　　　B：Sure, where is it?

:: 結構說明 Structure

　　XX 秀：「秀（xiù）」是英文「show」的音譯，意思是表演或展示，XX 可以
代入煙火、服裝、燈光、歌舞……等等各種表演類型的名詞。此外，「脫口秀」
是「talk show」的音譯，指的是一種談話性的表演節目。「作秀」原來是指演藝
人員登台演出，現在也用來指有意地做出某些言行舉止，來引起大眾的注意。
「走秀」是指模特兒穿時裝走在伸展台上展示。

　　XX xiù: "xiù" is transliterated from the English word "show", meaning performance
or display. XX can be various types of performance terms such as yānhuǒ 'fireworks',
fúzhuāng 'clothes i.e., fashion', dēngguāng 'lighting', gēwǔ 'singing and dancing', etc.
In addition, "tuōkǒuxiù" is transliterated from the English word "talk show", which
refers to the programs featuring talking performances. "zuò xiù" originally refers
to an entertainer who performs on stage. Now it is also used to denote someone
acting intentionally to catch the public's attention. "zǒu xiù" refers to models wearing
fashionable dresses while walking on the catwalk.

:: 合成詞與例句 Example　　　🎧 MP3-096

1 | **脫口秀**
　　那個小咖在網上做了一個脫口
　　秀，有很多人很喜歡看，然後
　　他就變大咖了。

1 | **tuōkǒuxiù**
　　That small potato did a talk show on
　　the Internet. A lot of people like to
　　watch it, and then he turned into a
　　big star.

2 | **作秀**

問題發生的時候，需要的是幫忙的人，不是作秀的人。

2 | **zuò xiù**

When a problem happens, it is people who help that are needed, not showmen.

3 | **走秀**

明天的服裝秀是七十幾歲的爺爺奶奶們穿最新的牛仔褲走秀，好像很有趣。

3 | **zǒu xiù**

Tomorrow's fashion show will feature grandpas and grandmas in their 70s walking in the latest jeans, which seems like a lot of fun.

❗ **你知道嗎 Do you know**

　　來自英文音譯的「秀」也有動詞的用法，意思是表現、展示，例如「很多人喜歡把旅遊的照片放在網上秀給大家看。」流行用語「秀下限」的意思是某個人的行為非常低級，展現出最壞的程度。這個詞除了用來嘲諷批評別人不文明的行為之外，更強調了差還要更差，差到沒有極限的感覺，所以語氣更為強烈，例如：「要是你的黑粉在網上寫了非常難聽的話，不用看他們秀下限，過好你自己的生活就好了。」

"xiù" is also used as a verb meaning to show or to display. For example, "Hěn duō rén xǐhuān bǎ lǚyóu de zhàopiàn fàng zài wǎng shàng xiù gěi dàjiā kàn. (Many people like to show travel pictures on the internet for people to see.)" The buzzword "xiù xiàxiàn 'display the low limit'" means that someone's behavior is nasty, as if displaying the worst level. In addition to criticizing someone's uncivilized behavior, the word emphasizes that the behavior is so bad that there seems to be no bottom line and the tone is very strong. For example, "Yàoshì nǐde hēifěn zài wǎng shàng xiě le fēicháng nántīng de huà, búyòng kàn tāmen xiù xiàxiàn, guò hǎo nǐ zìjǐ de shēnghuó jiù hǎo le. (If your anti-fans write horrible things on the Internet against you, you don't need to see them step over the line. Just move on with your life.)"

43 XX 趴 XX pā

:: **情境例句 Contextual Example**　　　　🎧 MP3-097

A：下個星期四是小明的生日，我
　　們幫他辦個生日趴，怎麼樣？

A： Next Thursday is Xiao Ming's
　　birthday. How about we throw a
　　birthday party for him?

B：好啊，還要找誰來呢？

B： Okay, who else should we invite?

:: **結構說明 Structure**

　　XX 趴：「趴（pā）」是英文「party」的音譯，意思是派對，一種社交聚會。XX 可以代入生日、聖誕、新年、睡衣等節日或是各種主題，和「趴」合起來就是某個節日或是為了某事、主題開的派對。「轟趴」是「home party」的音譯，指的是在家開的派對，「開趴」就是指開派對。

　　XX pā: "pā" is transliterated from the English word "party", meaning an informal social gathering. XX can be shēngrì 'birthday', shèngdàn 'Christmas', xīnnián 'New Year', shuìyī 'pajamas' and other holidays or various themes. Combining the words with "pā" means a party for some holiday, something or a theme. "hōngpā" is a transliteration for "home party", which refers to a party held at home, and "kāi pā" means to host a party.

:: **合成詞與例句 Example**　　　　🎧 MP3-098

1 | **聖誕趴**
你後天晚上要去參加公司辦的
聖誕趴嗎？

1 | **shèngdànpā**
Are you going to the company's
Christmas party the night after
tomorrow?

2 | **轟趴**
新搬來的鄰居常常開轟趴，吵
得我不能在家好好念書，好煩
喔。

2 | **hōngpā**
The new neighbors often throw
parties at home. It's so noisy that I
can't study at home. So annoying!

每年十二月三十一日這家餐廳
都會開趴慶祝新年的到來。你
今年想不想來？

Every year on December 31, this
restaurant holds a party to celebrate
the arrival of the New Year. Do you
want to come this year?

❗ 你知道嗎 Do you know

在台灣，百分比（%）的口語也說「趴」，例如 80% 可以讀作「百分之
八十」，口語上也有人說「八十趴」。這是因為百分比（%）在日語中讀作パー
セント（pāsento），擷取第一個音節就成了「趴」，而成為台語中眾多從日語
來的外來語之一，後來台語的「趴」再進一步進入台灣華語中。

In Taiwan, percentage (%) is also pronounced as "pā." For example, 80% can be read
as "bǎi fēn zhī bā shí." Some people also say "bā shí pā." This is because percentage
(%) is pronounced as パーセント (pāsento) in Japanese, and then the first syllable is
extracted to become "pā." It has become one of the many loan words from Japanese
to Taiwanese that later goes further into Táiwān Huáyǔ.

第五單元：外來語詞彙

PART V: Loan morphemes

I. 填空

Fill in the blank:

> a 粉絲　|　b 秀　|　c 趴

1 | 最近這幾年有不少年輕人喜歡找朋友在飯店開＿＿＿＿慶祝聖誕節，都不跟家人一起過了。

2 | 五月四日快到了，星戰（Star War）的＿＿＿＿們想好怎麼過了嗎？

3 | 下個星期五考完試，小林晚上在宿舍辦睡衣＿＿＿＿，我們一起去玩吧。

4 | 阿心是 BTS 的大＿＿＿＿，從 2013 年到現在他們的每一首歌她都會唱，你知道嗎？

5 | 巴黎（Paris）的歌舞＿＿＿＿已經有很長的歷史，如果你去法國旅遊一定要去看一次。

II. 對話配對
Conversation pairing:

1 ｜ 這位是你姐姐嗎？跟你長　　·
得好像啊。

2 ｜ 那邊怎麼把音樂開得那麼　　·
大聲呢？

3 ｜ 雖然他是個大咖，可是總　　·
是非常客氣。

4 ｜ 爺爺八十歲生日快到了，　　·
我們怎麼慶祝呢？

5 ｜ 明天我第一次走秀，好緊　　·
張啊。

· A ｜ 就是啊，我都被圈粉了。

· B ｜ 當然是辦個趴熱鬧一下
啊。

· C ｜ 這是我媽啦。你這麼會說
話，可以去上脫口秀節目
了。

· D ｜ 你就把看的人都當作西瓜
就好了，別擔心。

· E ｜ 可能是有人在開轟趴吧。

> ▶ 挑戰你自己：用「XX 粉／ XX 秀／ XX 趴」完成對話。
>
> Challenge yourself: Complete the dialogue with the word XX fěn / XX xiù / XX pā.

A：你知道馬友友（Yo Yo Ma）下個月要到台北來開音樂會嗎？

B：＿＿＿＿＿＿＿＿＿＿＿＿＿＿＿＿＿＿＿＿＿＿

:: **情境例句 Contextual Example**　🎧 MP3-100

A：日本一直是台灣人最喜歡去旅遊的國家，有的台灣人一年就要去日本好幾次。

B：這樣啊。最近日本也有「台灣熱」，到台灣旅遊的日本人比以前多，而且在日本只要有「台灣」兩個字的食物都賣得特別好。

A：Japan has always been the most popular country for Taiwanese to travel. Some Taiwanese go to Japan several times a year.

B：I see. Recently, Japan is also experiencing "Taiwan fever." There are more Japanese tourists visiting Taiwan than before, and foods labeled with the word "Taiwan" sell very well in Japan.

:: **結構說明 Structure**

　　XX 熱：「熱（rè）」是英文「fever」的翻譯，有為某事物瘋狂的意涵，意思是持續一段時期某種令人喜愛的潮流，XX 可以代入流行事物或活動的名詞，例如：台灣熱、中文熱、留學熱、珍珠奶茶熱。

　　XX rè: "rè" is transliterated from the English word "fever", having the sense of being crazy for something or some trend over a period of time. XX can be popular things or activities, such as Táiwānrè (Taiwan fever), Zhōngwénrè (Chinese fever), liúxuérè (study abroad fever), zhēnzhūnǎichárè (boba milk tea fever).

:: **合成詞與例句 Example**　🎧 MP3-101

1 | **中文熱**

大衛跟著中文熱開始學中文，到現在已經學了六年了。你可以跟他講中文。

1 | **Zhōngwénrè**

David started learning Chinese with the Chinese fever and has been learning it for six years now. You can speak with him in Chinese.

課本沒教的台灣華語句型50

2 | 留學熱

中國的留學熱讓很多有錢的父母都想把孩子送出國讀書，所以中國小留學生一年比一年多。

2 | liúxuérè

The fever of study abroad in China has made many rich parents want to send their children to study abroad. Therefore, the number of Chinese parachute kids is increasing every year.

3 | 珍珠奶茶熱

日本出現了不少有珍珠粉圓的奇怪食物，像是珍奶啤酒、珍奶餃子，這都是因為最近的珍珠奶茶熱。

3 | zhēnzhūnǎichárè

There are many strange foods with tapioca balls in Japan, such as tapioca beer and tapioca dumplings, all because of the recent boba milk tea fever.

! 你知道嗎 Do you know

和「XX 熱」相似的詞是「熱潮（rècháo）」，同樣在「熱潮」前面可以加上各種流行事物或活動的名詞，例如：運動健身熱潮、法國電影熱潮、買房熱潮。就像大海的潮汐一樣，「XX 熱潮」是可以重複出現的，但「XX 熱」一般是一次性的，過一段時間就會消失了。

The word similar to "XX rè" is "rècháo 'upsurge'." You can also add various popular things or activities in front of "rècháo", such as yùndòng jiànshēn rècháo (fitness boom), fàguó diànyǐng rècháo (French movie boom), and mǎifáng rècháo (house buying boom). Just like ocean waves, "XX rècháo" can be repeated, but "XX rè" is generally one-time and will disappear after a period of time.

45

XX 門 XX mén

:: **情境例句 Contextual Example**　　🎧 MP3-102

A：你知道三星「寫手門」嗎？

B：知道啊，從那以後，我就不看網上別人寫的手機試用報告了。

A：Do you know Samsung's "Fake-web-reviews-gate"?

B：Yes, I know. Since then, I have not read others' mobile phone trial reports on the Internet anymore.

:: **結構說明 Structure**

　　XX 門：1972 年美國發生了民主黨辦公室被闖入的水門案（Watergate scandal），從那以後美國政治界或是大企業發生的醜聞都被叫做「XX 門」，例如：台灣三星公司（Samsung）花錢請人假裝是網友分享手機使用心得的「寫手門」、福斯汽車公司（Volkswagen）在使用柴油引擎的車上裝置特別的軟體來通過美國廢氣排放標準的「柴油門」、希拉蕊‧柯林頓（Hillary Clinton）用自己的私人電郵帳號進行公務通信的「電郵門」、川普（Trump）被指涉及俄羅斯影響 2016 年美國總統大選的「通俄門」。

　　XX mén: In 1972, the Watergate scandal happened in the United States. The Democratic Party's office was broken into. Since then, scandals in American politics or big corporations have been called "XX mén (XX gate)." For example, Taiwan's Samsung Fake-web-reviews-gate, in which the company hired writers to pretend to be customers and shared their mobile phone user's experience on websites. Dieselgate (or Emissionsgate) was when Volkswagen installed special software in their diesel engine cars to pass US exhaust emission standards. Emailgate was because Hillary Clinton used her personal email account for official communications. In Russiagate, Trump was accused of being involved in the Russian interference in the 2016 U.S. presidential election.

1 | **柴油門**
　我本來開德國車，發生了「柴油門」以後，就換日本車了。

1 | **Cháiyóumén**
　I used to drive a German car. After Emissionsgate happened, I changed to a Japanese car.

2 | **電郵門**
　「電郵門」讓有些人不相信希拉蕊能管理好國家大事。

2 | **Diànyóumén**
　Emailgate made some people disbelieve in Hillary's ability to manage national affairs.

3 | **通俄門**
　因為「通俄門」，很多人開始注意外國影響美國總統選舉的可能。

3 | **Tōngèmén**
　Because of Russiagate, many people began to pay attention to the possibility of foreign influence on American presidential elections.

❗ **你知道嗎 Do you know**

　　有兩個常用詞跟「水門」一樣，雖然有「門」字，但都沒有「門」的意思，一個是「冷門」，是不受歡迎、被忽視、很少人知道的意思，另一個是跟「冷門」相反的「熱門」，意思是非常受歡迎、引起大家討論的，兩個詞都可以用來形容事物，例如：冷門的職業、冷門的新聞、熱門的電視節目、熱門的旅遊地點。

　　There are two commonly used words like "shuǐmén" which doesn't have anything to do with the literal "mén 'gate / door'." One is "lěngmén 'cold door,'" meaning unpopular, being neglected, or not commonly known. The other is an antonym of lěngmén, "rèmén 'hot door,'" meaning very popular and discussion-raising. Both words can be used as stative verbs, such as lěngmén de zhíyè (unpopular occupation), lěngmén de xīnwén (unpopular news), rèmén de diànshì jiémù (popular TV program), and rèmén de lǚyóu dìdiǎn (popular tourist destination).

XX 風 XX fēng

:: **情境例句 Contextual Example** 🎧 MP3-104

A：這個送給你，是我從日本帶回來的。

B：哇！和風的杯子，謝謝你。我很喜歡。

A：This is for you. I brought it back from Japan.

B：Wow! Japanese style cup. Thank you. I like it very much.

:: **結構說明 Structure**

　　XX 風：「風（fēng）」這裡的意思是風格或樣式，日語「和風（わふう）」指的是日本風格，中文也用這個詞，讀作 héfēng。從「和風」類推，XX 可以代入國家、地域、時代……等等名詞來表示某種風格，例如：中國風、北歐風、運動風。「XX 風」可以用來形容商品、服飾、建築、室內設計、音樂。

　　XX fēng: "fēng 'wind'" here means style. Japanese " わ ふ う (wafuu)" refers to Japanese style. This word is also used in Chinese and pronounced as héfēng. By analogy with "héfēng", XX can be nouns of country, region, era, etc. to express a certain style, e.g., Zhōngguófēng (Chinese style), Běi'ōufēng (Nordic style), yùndòngfēng (sports style). "XX fēng" can be used to describe commodities, clothing, architecture, interior design, and music.

:: **合成詞與例句 Example** 🎧 MP3-105

1 | **中國風**

這家茶館總是放中國風的音樂，讓人感覺好像茶更香了。

1 | **Zhōngguófēng**

This teahouse always plays Chinese style music, which makes people feel as if the tea is more fragrant.

2 | **北歐風**

我喜歡北歐風的家具，簡簡單單，一看就覺得很舒服。

2 | **Běi'ōufēng**

I like the Nordic style furniture. It's very simple. You will feel very comfortable once you see it.

3 ｜ 運動風

我就愛穿運動風的衣服，連上班都這麼穿。還好老闆沒說不可以。

3 ｜ yùndòngfēng

I love to wear sporty clothes very much, even for work. Luckily, the boss didn't say not ok.

❗ 你知道嗎 Do you know

　　除了「和風料理」（日式飲食）以外，一般用「XX 式（shì）」來形容不同種類的餐飲，例如：西式早餐、港式點心、韓式泡菜。這裡的「式」是方法或是樣子的意思。XX 可以代入國家、地域、人名、物品、時代等名詞，除了用來形容餐飲，也用在形容活動、行為，例如：台（灣）式管理、南歐式生活、洋蔥式穿法。至於商品、服裝、建築，除了可以用「XX 風」，也可以用「XX 式」。

　　Except for "héfēng liàolǐ (Japanese cuisine)", "XX-shì (style)" is generally used to describe different kinds of cuisine, such as xīshì zǎocān (western breakfast), gǎngshì diǎnxīn (Hong Kong dim sum), and hánshì pàocài (Korean kimchi). "shì" here means method or appearance. XX can be nouns of country, region, person's name, object, and time. In addition to describing cuisine, it is used to describe activities and behaviors, such as Tái(wān) shì guǎnlǐ (Taiwanese way of management), Nánōushì shēnghuó (southern European lifestyle), yángcōngshì chuānfǎ (onion-style dressing i.e., dressing in layers). As for commodity, clothing, and buildings, both "XX fēng" and "XX shì" are acceptable.

47　XX 族 XX zú

:: **情境例句 Contextual Example**　　　　🎧 MP3-106

A：你昨天晚上沒睡好嗎？怎麼看
　　起來這麼累？

B：唉，昨天晚上十二點半的時
　　候，有飆車族在我家附近。把
　　我吵起來，氣死我了！

A：Did you not sleep well last night?
　　Why do you look so tired?

B：Sigh. At 12:30 last night, I was
　　awakened by street racing in my
　　neighborhood. I was so mad.

:: **結構說明 Structure**

　　XX 族：「族」這裡的意思是有相同屬性的人們。日語「暴走族」（ぼうそうぞく）指的是一群喜歡騎改裝摩托車的年輕人，他們經常把機車的消音器移除，騎在路上發出巨大噪音，並且不遵守交通規則。這種文化在 1986 年傳到台灣造就了相似的「飆車族」。從「飆車族」類推，XX 可以代入各種屬性的名詞，例如：「上班族」就是領固定薪水的人們，「公車族」就是坐公車上班、上學的人們，「低頭族」就是常常低頭使用手機、平板電腦的人們。

　　XX zú: "zú 'clan'" means people with the same attributes. In Japanese, "ぼ う そ う ぞ く (Bōsōzoku)" refers to a group of young people who like to ride modified motorcycles. They often remove the muffler from their motorcycles, make loud noises while riding on the road, and do not follow the traffic rules. This kind of culture spread to Taiwan in 1986 and made a similar "biāochēzú (motor racing clan)." By analogy with "biāochēzú", XX can be terms of various attributes, e.g., "shàngbānzú" are people with a fixed salary, "gōngchēzú" are people who go to work or school by bus, and "dītóuzú" are people who often have their heads down and use mobile phones or tablets.

1 | **上班族**

上班族一般九點上班，五點下班。有的人下了班以後還要去上課，真辛苦。

1 | **shàngbānzú**

Salarymen usually go to work at nine and get off work at five. Some people have to go to class after work, which is really tough.

2 | **公車族**

公車族最怕坐在窗邊的位子，到快下車的時候，旁邊的人正在睡覺。

2 | **gōngchēzú**

What worried the bus commuters the most is that when they sit by the window and are about to get off, the next person is sleeping.

3 | **低頭族**

低頭族要多注意脖子和眼睛的健康，應該每四十分鐘就休息五分鐘。

3 | **dītóuzú**

Phubbers must pay more attention to the health of their neck and eyes. They should take a five-minute break every forty minutes.

❗ **你知道嗎 Do you know**

「家族」是指有血緣關係的同姓親屬，「民族」是指有共同血緣、共同語言、共同生活習俗的群體。在十七世紀漢民族移居台灣以前，台灣已經有許多原住民族生活於此，這些原住民族與南太平洋島嶼的原住民族系出同源，同屬南島語族。經過基因檢測，已經證實紐西蘭的毛利人與台灣的阿美族有血緣關係，他們也有相同的文化和相似的語言。

"jiāzú" refers to blood relatives of the same surname. "mínzú" refers to a group who share the same ties by blood, language, and customs. Before the Han people immigrated to Taiwan in the 17th century, there were already many aborigines living in Taiwan. These aborigines have the same origin as those from the South Pacific Islands and belong to the Austronesian group. After genetic testing, it has been confirmed that the Māori in New Zealand are related to the Amis in Taiwan, and they also share the same culture and similar languages.

第五單元：外來語詞彙

PART V: Loan morphemes

I. 填空

Fill in the blank:

a 熱　|　b 門　|　c 風　|　d 族

1｜我弟弟是個夜貓＿＿＿＿，總是玩電腦玩到半夜兩三點才去睡覺。

2｜像通俄＿＿＿＿那樣的事可能發生在美國，也可能發生在其他國家。

3｜在美國，有一些中學和小學開了中文課，是因為十多年前的中文＿＿＿＿。現在還有嗎？

4｜我喜歡在下雨的時候穿著我的英國＿＿＿＿外套去上班，心情就變好了。

5｜開車＿＿＿＿都應該記住而且一定要做到「喝酒不開車，開車不喝酒」。

II. 對話配對
Conversation pairing:

1 | 今天要去參加什麼表演嗎？怎麼穿得這麼西部牛仔風？

2 | 「寫手門」以後，你覺得還會有公司花錢請人在網上說自己商品的好話嗎？

3 | 那家飲料店外面為什麼有那麼多人在排隊啊？

4 | 今天頭髮想怎麼剪呢？

5 | 放三天假打算做什麼呢？

A | 可能不會了吧。被發現的話就完了。

B | 學生風，看起來比較年輕。

C | 能去旅遊的地方都是人，還是在家做低頭族上網看電影吧。

D | 不是，是今天晚上要去一個朋友的生日趴，想穿得特別一點。

E | 那些人都是為了喝珍珠奶茶，聽說有人排六個小時呢。這就是珍奶熱了吧。

> ▶ 挑戰你自己：用「XX 熱／XX 風／XX 族」完成對話。
> Challenge yourself: Complete the dialogue with XX rè / XX fēng / XX zú.

A：昨天的聖誕趴有好幾個小女孩穿得像《冰雪奇緣》（Frozen）的艾莎 (Elsa)，很可愛。

B：_____

48 XX 控 XX kòng

:: **情境例句 Contextual Example**　　　🎧 MP3-109

A：每次見到阿明，他總是穿著牛
　　仔褲，而且每條都不一樣，真
　　是個牛仔褲控。

B：是啊，我聽說他有三十幾條牛
　　仔褲呢。

A：Every time I see A Ming, he always
　　wears jeans, and every pair is
　　different. He's really a jeansaholic.

B：Yeah. I heard he has more than 30
　　pairs of jeans.

:: **結構說明 Structure**

　　XX 控：「控（kòng）」在這裡的用法來自日語外來詞「ロリコン」，中文
音譯為「蘿莉控」，指的是喜好動漫作品中幼小女孩角色的人。現在 XX 可以帶
入任何名詞，指的是非常喜歡 XX 的人，例如：牛仔褲控、藍色控、旅遊控、冰
淇淋控。

　　XX kòng: The usage of "kòng 'control'" here comes from the Japanese loan word
"ロリコン (rolikon)", which is transliterated in Mandarin as "luólìkòng" referring
to the people who like young girl characters in Japanese anime. Now XX can be any
term to refer to the people who like XX very much, such as niúzǎikùkòng (jeansaholic),
lánsèkòng (blueholic), lǚyóukòng (travelholic), and bīngqílínkòng (ice-creamaholic).

:: **合成詞與例句 Example**　　　🎧 MP3-110

1 | **藍色控**
　　我姐姐是個藍色控，什麼東西
　　都買藍色的。

1 | **lánsèkòng**
　　My sister is a blueholic. Everything
　　she buys is in blue.

2 | **旅遊控**
　　他的護照兩年換過三次，所有
　　的朋友都相信他是個旅遊控。

2 | **lǚyóukòng**
　　His passport was renewed three
　　times in two years. All his friends
　　believe that he is a travelholic.

3 | **冰淇淋控**

冰淇淋控一定要看這個網站，
全部都在介紹冰淇淋店。

3 | **bīngqílínkòng**

Ice-creamaholics must read this website. The whole site is about ice cream stores.

❗ 原來如此 No wonder

「蘿莉」一詞來自納博科夫（Nabokov）的小說《蘿莉塔》（Lolita），書中描述一個中年男子愛上一個十二歲的小女孩。現在心理學所說的蘿莉塔情結（Lolita Complex），指的就是極度喜歡未成年女孩的傾向，也就是「蘿莉控」一詞的來源。

The word "luólì" comes from Nabokov's novel *Lolita* which describes a middle-aged man falling in love with a twelve-year-old girl. The Lolita Complex in psychology now refers to the tendency to like underage girls. That's where "luólìkòng" comes from.

:: 情境例句 Contextual Example　　　🎧 MP3-111

A：好久不見啊，小林。

B：為了考試，當了三個月宅男，
　　今天終於可以出門了。

A：Long time no see, Xiao Lin.

B：After three months of being an otaku
　　for the exam, I finally got to go out
　　today.

:: 結構說明 Structure

　　宅 X：「宅（zhái）」的意思是居住的地方。日語「御宅（おたく）」指的是喜好電玩、動漫、上網且經常待在家裡的人。這個詞傳到台灣讓那些經常待在家或宿舍不出門、不常與人社交的男網友也自稱自己是「宅男」，後來還出現「宅女」。另外「宅配」、「宅急便」是直接從日語的漢字進入中文的詞彙，意思分別是送貨和快遞送貨到家。

　　zhái X: "zhái 'residence'" means a place to live. In Japanese, "お た く (Otaku)" refers to people who like video games, animation, surfing online, and often stay at home. The word spread to Taiwan later. Male netizens in Taiwan who often stay at home or do not go out from the dormitory and do not often socialize with others also call themselves "zháinán (male homebody)." Later "zháinǚ (female homebody)" was invented. In addition to that, "zháipèi" and "zháijíbiàn" are imported directly from Japanese, using the same characters, meaning delivery and home express delivery, respectively.

:: 合成詞與例句 Example　　　🎧 MP3-112

1 | **宅女**
我要經常去旅行，交很多朋友，不要做宅女。

1 | **zháinǚ**
I want to travel a lot, make a lot of friends, and not be a shut-in (woman).

2 | 宅配

從機場拉這麼多行李搭火車，然後還要換公車，太不方便了，還是宅配到旅館去吧。

2 | zháipèi

It's too inconvenient to pull so much luggage from the airport, take the train, and then transfer to the bus. Let's have the luggage delivered to the hotel instead.

3 | 宅急便

林小姐明天就要出國，你還是用宅急便把她的護照寄給她吧。

3 | zháijíbiàn

Miss Lin is going abroad tomorrow. You had better send her passport by express delivery.

❗ 你知道嗎 Do you know

「宅」也有動詞的用法，例如「宅在家」。要是一個人經常在家、不喜歡外出社交，也可以說「這個人很宅」。雖然日語中說一個人是「御宅」有負面評價的意思，但是台灣華語中的「宅男」、「宅女」並沒有太負面的意思，只是指不常外出的特質，最近還有人自稱是「宅爸、宅媽、阿宅」。

"zhái" is also used as a verb, such as "zhái zài jiā (stay at home)." If a person often stays at home and doesn't like going out to socialize, you can also say "Zhè ge rén hěn zhái. (This person is a homebody)." If you say that a person is an "otaku" in Japanese, it has a negative connotation. However, zháiná and zháinǔ in Táiwān Huáyǔ do not have a negative connotation. They just refer to the characteristic of a person who does not go out often. Recently, some people claim themselves to be zháibà (home-dad), zháimā (home-mom), or āzhái (homebody).

:: 情境例句 Contextual Example　　　　🎧 MP3-113

A：最近心情不好，上星期去日本
　　爆買了好幾十萬的東西。

A：Recently, I was in a bad mood. I
　　went to Japan last week and bought
　　a lot of things costing hundreds of
　　thousands.

B：錢包瘦了，心情好了吧？

B：Your wallet is thinner. Do you feel
　　better now?

:: 結構說明 Structure

　　爆 X：「爆（bào）」這裡是描述突然且大量發生的行為。日語「爆買い（ば
くがい）」指的是大量購買商品的行為。2014 年起出現了中國觀光客到日本大
買日本製商品的現象，因此新聞媒體開始出現這個詞。這個詞後來也傳入台灣
華語，並在台灣類推產生更多「爆 X」的詞彙。X 可以代入動作動詞或狀態動詞，
所以有表示猛烈毆打的「爆打」、表示突然非常生氣的「爆氣」，以及表示突
然大吃的「爆吃」等詞。

bào X: "bào 'explosive'" here is used to describe the behavior that occurs suddenly
and a lot. In Japanese, "ばくがい (bokugai)" refers to the behavior of buying goods in
large quantities. Since 2014, there has been a phenomenon of Chinese tourists visiting
Japan to buy a lot of Japanese-made goods, and the news media began to use this
term to describe it. This word was later introduced into Táiwān Huáyǔ and generate
more words of "bào X" by analogy. X can be action verbs or stative verbs. Therefore,
"bàodǎ (explosive beating)" means violent beating, "bàoqì (explosive anger)" means
suddenly getting very angry, and "bàochī (explosive eating)" means eating a lot in a
short time.

1 | **爆打**

阿金的電腦又不動了，你可以去告訴他爆打電腦也沒用嗎？很吵耶。

1 | **bàodǎ**

A Jin's computer is frozen again. Can you go tell him that it is useless to blow up the computer? It's noisy!

2 | **爆氣**

別跟小麗說她前男友的事，她一聽到前男友的名字就爆氣。

2 | **bàoqì**

Don't tell Xiao Li anything about her ex-boyfriend. She gets mad when she hears his name.

3 | **爆吃**

新年放了好幾天假，我都在家爆吃，怎麼會不胖呢？

3 | **bàochī**

The New Year's holiday came with several days off. I just stayed home and ate a lot. How could I not gain weight?

! **你知道嗎 Do you know**

「爆」也有「爆炸」的意思，新聞媒體上經常出現「X爆」的詞組來形容某種極端情況的發生，是「X到爆炸」的縮略，X也可以代入動作動詞或狀態動詞，例如：怕爆、刷爆、擠爆，意思分別是非常害怕、刷卡消費超過上限、人多非常擁擠。

"bào" also means "bàozhà 'explode'." The phrase "X bào" often appears in the news media to describe the occurrence of some extreme situation. It is an abbreviation of "X dào bàozhà (X to explode)". X can also be action verbs or stative verbs, such as pàbào, shuābào, and jǐbào, which mean being very scared, maxing out a credit card, and extremely crowded respectively.

I. 填空

Fill in the blank:

> a 控　|　b 宅　|　c 爆

1｜心情不好就 _____ 吃，是很不健康的。我們出去走走吧。

2｜我弟弟就是個 _____ 男，放假就只會在家，哪裡都不想去。

3｜我妹妹是個水果 _____ ，可以只吃水果不吃飯。夏天水果多，她最開心了。

4｜現在出國旅遊 _____ 買的人已經比以前少多了，因為網路上什麼都買得到。

5｜小紅最愛買帽子，朋友們都知道她是個帽子 _____ 。你送她帽子就對了。

II. 對話配對
Conversation pairing:

1 | 這兩張沙發價錢差不多，買哪張好呢？ ·

2 | 聽說六十二趴的男生喜歡戴眼鏡的女生。 ·

3 | 昨天晚上我玩網上的遊戲，玩了三個多小時，差一點點就贏了。 ·

4 | 現在買什麼都可以宅配，青菜、魚肉、水果什麼都可以。 ·

5 | 我昨天去看了一部電影，讓我爆哭，差一點走不出電影院。 ·

· A | 就是這麼方便，讓年輕人容易變阿宅。

· B | 喔？那你有沒有爆氣？

· C | 真的嗎？眼鏡控的男生這麼多啊？

· D | 是什麼樣的故事讓你這麼傷心難過啊？說來聽聽吧。

· E | 我是綠色控。如果是我，一定買綠的那張。

挑戰你自己：用「XX 控／宅 X／爆 X」完成對話。
Challenge yourself: Complete the dialogue with the word XX kòng / zhái X / bào X.

A：哇！一、二、三……十六、十七、十八，你怎麼有這麼多鞋子啊？

B：＿＿＿＿＿＿＿＿＿＿＿＿＿＿＿＿＿＿＿＿＿

第五單元：外來語詞彙　PART V: Loan morphemes

練習一 Exercise 1

Section I

1 他那麼想去，就給他帶去吧。

2 我今天才發現說大房子打掃起來又累又花時間。

3 她非常喜歡吃水果，不管吃得多飽，什麼水果都還能給他吃下去。

4 台北的交通哪有說很不方便？

5 阿新小學的時候有打籃球，所以現在特別高。

6 每天洗完臉以後，用這一瓶，三個月以後就能給你年輕五歲。

7 我們公司要不要參加這個計畫，你星期四要給老闆報告。

8 公園離這裡沒有說很遠，走路就能到了。

9 我有參觀過你們學校了，我就在學校的書店等你吧。

10 那個座位是給老人或者不方便的人坐的。

Section II

1 d   2 e   3 a   4 b, c

練習二 Exercise 2

Section I

1 a   2 b   3 b   4 a   5 a

Section II

1 c   2 a   3 b   4 a   5 c   6 a

練習三 Exercise 3

Section I

1 最近報告很多，今天一進教室老師就給我們考試，還好我昨天晚上有讀到書。

2 你看這個東西掛在那兒會不會太高（了）？

3 我開了半個小時，這門還是開不起來！

4 對電腦的麻煩我很有經驗，你電腦的問題我可以檢查看看。

5 跑了十公里，現在真的餓到了。

6 那麼多漢堡、飲料用這個袋子真的裝得起來嗎？

Section II

1 e   2 a   3 b   4 d   5 a   6 e   7 c

練習四 Exercise 4

Section I

1 c   2 d   3 b   4 c   5 a / b

Section II

1 ❶   2 ❷   3 ❷   4 ❶

解答
Answer Key

課本沒教的台灣華語句型50

練習五 Exercise 5

Section I

1 b **2** d **3** a **4** c **5** c

Section II

1 ❷ **2** ❷ **3** ❶ **4** ❷

練習六 Exercise 6

Section I

1 a **2** c **3** b **4** a **5** b

Section II

1 ❷ **2** ❶ **3** ❷ **4** ❶

練習七 Exercise 7

Section I

1 b **2** e **3** d **4** a **5** c

Section II

1（1）-（C）**2**（2）-（D）**3**（3）-（E）**4**（4）-（A）**5**（5）-（B）

練習八 Exercise 8

Section I

1 c　　2 a　　3 d　　4 b　　5 a

Section II

1 (1) - (C)　2 (2) - (E)　3 (3) - (B)　4 (4) - (D)　5 (1) - (A)

練習九 Exercise 9

Section I

1 b　　2 d　　3 a　　4 b　　5 c

Section II

1 (1) - (E)　2 (2) - (A)　3 (3) - (C)　4 (4) - (D)　5 (5) - (B)

練習十 Exercise 10

Section I

1 c　　2 e　　3 b　　4 a　　5 d

Section II

1 ❶　　2 ❷　　3 ❶　　4 ❶　　5 ❷

解答
Answer Key

練習十一 Exercise 11

Section I

1 c　　2 e　　3 d　　4 a　　5 b

Section II

1 ❷　　2 ❶　　3 ❶　　4 ❶　　5 ❷

練習十二 Exercise 12

Section I

1 d　　2 e　　3 b　　4 c　　5 a

Section II

1 ❶　　2 ❷　　3 ❷　　4 ❶　　5 ❶

練習十三 Exercise 13

Section I

1 c　　2 a　　3 c　　4 a　　5 b

Section II

1 （1）-（C）　2 （2）-（E）　3 （3）-（A）　4 （4）-（B）　5 （5）-（D）

練習十四 Exercise 14

Section I

1 d **2** b **3** a **4** c **5** d

Section II

1 (1)-(D) **2** (2)-(A) **3** (3)-(E) **4** (4)-(B) **5** (5)-(C)

練習十五 Exercise 15

Section I

1 c **2** b **3** a **4** c **5** a

Section II

1 (1)-(E) **2** (2)-(C) **3** (3)-(B) **4** (4)-(A) **5** (5)-(D)

索引
Index

索引
Index

索引
Index

索引
Index

國家圖書館出版品預行編目資料

Taiwan Mandarin: 50 Patterns Not in Your Textbook
課本沒教的台灣華語句型 50 全新修訂版 / 蔡佩庭著
-- 修訂初版 -- 臺北市：瑞蘭國際 , 2023.06
208 面；17 × 23 公分 -- （語文館；06）
ISBN：978-626-7274-33-0（平裝）
1. CST：漢語語法 2. CST：句法

802.633   112008585

語文館 06
Taiwan Mandarin:
50 Patterns Not in Your Textbook
課本沒教的台灣華語句型 50 全新修訂版

作者｜蔡佩庭
責任編輯｜鄧元婷、王愿琦、葉仲芸
校對｜蔡佩庭、鄧元婷、王愿琦、葉仲芸

華語錄音｜林銘珊、徐家偉
錄音室｜采漾錄音製作有限公司
封面設計、版型設計及內文排版｜格瓦尤

瑞蘭國際出版

董事長｜張暖彗
社長兼總編輯｜王愿琦

編輯部
副總編輯｜葉仲芸
主編｜潘治婷
設計部主任｜陳如琪

業務部
經理｜楊米琪
主任｜林湲洵
組長｜張毓庭

出版社｜瑞蘭國際有限公司
地址｜台北市大安區安和路一段 104 號 7 樓之一
電話｜(02)2700-4625 ‧ 傳真｜(02)2700-4622
訂購專線｜(02)2700-4625
劃撥帳號｜19914152 瑞蘭國際有限公司
瑞蘭國際網路書城｜www.genki-japan.com.tw

法律顧問｜海灣國際法律事務所　呂錦峯律師

總經銷｜聯合發行股份有限公司
電話｜(02)2917-8022、2917-8042
傳真｜(02)2915-6275、2915-7212
印刷｜科億印刷股份有限公司
出版日期｜2023 年 06 月初版 1 刷
定價｜480 元
ISBN｜978-626-7274-33-0